N.Z. LISTENER SHORT STORIES

N.Z. Listener
Short Stories

chosen by

BILL MANHIRE

METHUEN
NEW ZEALAND

First published in 1977 by
Methuen Publications (NZ) Ltd,
238 Wakefield Street, Wellington.

456 02270 8

Printed by Wright & Carman Ltd,
Trentham

Cover painting: 'Anita' by Pamela Wolfe

Acknowledgements

The editor is grateful to the following writers, copyright holders, and publishers for permission to reprint stories in this anthology: Frank Sargeson and Longman Paul for 'Two Worlds' and 'Showers' (from *The Stories of Frank Sargeson,* 1973), and to Frank Sargeson for 'Making Father Pay'; to Roderick Finlayson and Auckland University Press for 'The Everlasting Miracle' (from *Brown Man's Burden and Later Stories,* 1973); to A. P. Gaskell and Auckland University Press for 'The Big Game' (from *The Big Game and Other Stories,* 1977); to R. A. Copland for 'Yes, to the Very End'; to Barbara Duggan for Maurice Duggan's 'A Small Story' and 'Race Day' (from *Immanuel's Land,* Pilgrim Press, 1956); to Helen Shaw for 'The Bull' (from *The Orange Tree and Other Stories,* Pelorus Press, 1957); to Janet Frame for 'Lolly-Legs'; to Phillip Wilson for 'One World' (from *Some are Lucky,* Denis Glover, 1960); to Noel Hilliard for 'Aunty Wai's Wedding' (from *A Piece of Land,* Robert Hale, 1963); to Dennis McEldowney for 'The Mayor and Mrs McBride'; to Albert Wendt for 'The Dark Angel'; to Joy Cowley for 'The Silk' and 'Rural Delivery'; to Witi Ihimaera for 'The Liar', and to Witi Ihimaera and Heinemann for 'The Child' (from *Pounamu Pounamu,* 1972); to J. Edward Brown for 'What Did You Do in the War, Daddy?'; to Patricia Grace and Longman Paul for 'Holiday' (from *Waiariki,* 1975); to Maurice Gee and Auckland University Press for 'A Glorious Morning, Comrade' (from *A Glorious Morning, Comrade,* 1975); to Kerry A. L. Hulme for 'King Bait'; to Barry Mitcalfe and Outrigger Publishers for 'I Say, Wait for Me' (from *I Say, Wait for Me,* 1976); to Hone Tuwhare for 'Pigeons' (to be published in *Making a Fist of It,* Jackstraw Press); and to A. K. Grant for 'An Inquiry into the Construction and Classification of the New Zealand Short Story'.

Particular thanks are also due to the *Listener* for assistance in researching the stories for this selection.

Contents

Notes on the Selection

The only virtue A. R. D. Fairburn felt able to ascribe to short stories—and to very short ones at that—was that 'they do leave you time to weed the cabbages and give the lawn a bit of a once-over'. On such evidence one might be forgiven for thinking that readers of the *Listener,* where Fairburn made his pronouncement, must be avid gardeners. Since the magazine first appeared in 1939 it has printed something like 1,000 stories, many of them among the finest written in this country.

This book is not intended to be a nostalgic journey through the pages of the *Listener.* Readers will find many familiar names missing, some purely for reasons of space, others because their stories were perfectly judged for a weekly journal: delightful on first acquaintance, but the charm has vanished on subsequent encounters. In making a selection, I have simply chosen from among the stories I liked best and wanted to return to.

I have, however, kept two considerations in mind. First, it seemed important to acknowledge the fact that the *Listener* has been publishing stories for nearly forty years. So, in some limited sense, this is a 'historical' selection. The first story here appeared in 1941, the last in 1976; the stories are printed in chronological order—with the single exception of A. K. Grant's 'Inquiry', which looked as if it would be happy to have the last word. Second, I wanted the selection to reflect something of the variety of stories printed in the *Listener.*

Yet this last has not been easy. A few years ago, a reader wrote to the *Listener* to register his disappointment at its choice of stories. 'So many of them,' he said, 'seem to deal with depressing or reflective topics—nostalgia, old age, and failures of the suburban life-style.' And this is true. The very best *Listener* stories are not happy affairs. By and large they offer a world of diminished possibilities, tending to see points of growth in human experience as moments of loss or damage. If one were to accept the critical truism that New Zealand authors write well and often about children, one would also have to say that they write as well and as often about the old, the lonely, the emotionally destitute.

The *Listener* has printed many light-hearted pieces, of course. But good comic writing, writing able to go on surprising the reader after repeated encounters, is as hard to come by in the pages of the *Listener* as elsewhere. What the lighter pieces included here share with those less happy, is an underlying commitment—a commitment not primarily to 'issues' or to the craft of fiction, but to the characters and feelings being portrayed. There is a world of difference between the ecological splutterings of Mrs McBride in Dennis McEldowney's tale and the remarkable piece of poetry which the dying wife in Albert Wendt's 'The Dark Angel' addresses to her husband. Yet as moments of address, they are both parts of a single world—a world in which human emotion is attended to with serious respect.

Witi Ihimaera—whose first published story, 'The Liar', is printed here—has said that he is concerned in his work to describe emotional landscapes, landscapes of the heart. I suppose that such descriptions are what we finally look for in any piece of literature, and for my own part, I believe that all the stories I have chosen are worth returning to for such descriptions. None of them, that is, merely accommodate human feelings within a nice 3,000 words; in their various ways—even in irony or horrified delight—they declare themselves on behalf of the emotions they describe.

BILL MANHIRE

July 1977

Two Worlds

FRANK SARGESON

My granpa Munro was a Belfast man. He was also a Loyal Orangeman, and I think I first became aware of these facts when I asked why granpa was dressed in a fancy apron in a photograph that hung on the wall. Granma explained to me, but I was too young to have much idea what it all meant.

Then one time during school holidays, when my brother and I were staying with granma and granpa Munro, we found a string of beads in the street. I say we, but my brother said he saw it first. I said I did.

Neither of us had ever before seen such a string of beads. Instead of their being all of an even size, or else threaded so that they began small and grew large and then got small again, this string was made of a number of small beads that were interrupted at regular intervals by a big one. We counted the number of big beads and the number of small ones in between, and the number altogether, and this kept us busy for quite a time. Then we squabbled over who was to be the owner, but my brother was the older, he had the advantage of me, and the findings disappeared into his pocket.

I got my own back by saying they weren't worth anything anyhow. And as soon as we were home I said that we'd found something, and told my brother to show granma. He gave me a look that told me plainly what he thought of me but he brought the beads out, and granma hardly had them in her hand when she gave a sort of groan and dropped them on the table. She spread out her arms to keep us from going near, and granpa got up from his chair and looked at the beads over the top of his glasses. Granma said we were not to touch and she took the tongs and would have put the beads in the fire if granpa hadn't stopped her.

Well, granma went on getting the tea, we asked her what the beads were and she said they were a Catholic thing. I don't think that meant a great deal to us. We knew what Catholic churches looked like from the outside and that was about all, though at school we'd learned to say a rhyme:

Catholic dogs don't like frogs,
And won't eat meat on Friday.

Meantime granpa was walking up and down, stopping now and then to look at the beads. I suppose there must have been quite a tug of war going on between the man who was a Loyal Orangeman, and the man who didn't want to do anything dishonest. Finally he pushed the beads on to a piece of paper with one finger, and put them on the mantlepiece.

I don't think we thought about the beads for very long that evening. My main feeling about them was quite a satisfactory one. My brother had prevented me from being able to say they were mine, now he couldn't say they were his either. I felt that we were quits.

When we came home from going to the butcher's for granma the next morning we found that granpa had the horse harnessed in the buggy, and was waiting to take us for a drive. We ran and put our boots and stockings on, which was the rule whenever we went out driving, then we climbed up and sat beside granpa. He touched Beauty with the whip, and driving out the gate we waved to granma who was standing at the door to watch us go.

Granpa turned in the direction of the main street, and at the corner a man was lighting his pipe in the middle of the road.

By your leave! granpa shouted out, and he made the man jump. But my brother and I turned round and saw him laughing, and we knew it was mainly because of the straw hat, with holes for his ears to stick through, that Beauty wore. On hot days granpa always put it on, and it was supposed to keep him from getting sunstroke.

All the way along the main street granpa shouted out, By your leave! to people that were crossing the street, even though it didn't look as if any of them were going to be run over. And my brother and I saw so many people laughing that we felt a little shy and uncomfortable until we were through to the other end of the town.

It was a part of the town we didn't know very well, the houses were smaller and closer together than in the part we knew, though granpa pulled up outside a big house with a lawn and trees in front. He gave us the paper that he had wrapped the beads in, and told us we were to go and knock at the front door and ask for Mr Doyle. When Mr Doyle came to the door we were to say we'd found some beads, give him the parcel, and come straight back again.

We went up a path that wound through the trees and took us out of sight of the street, and when we knocked at the door it was opened by a fat lady with a red face.

Please is Mister Doyle in? my brother said.

Mister Doyle? the fat lady said, and we were frightened by the way she looked down at us.

Do you mean the Very Reverend Dean Doyle? she said, and what she said made us more frightened. I looked at my brother, my brother looked at me. Neither of us had a voice any more.

Then a voice from behind the fat lady said, Well boys?

The fat lady stepped back and in her place was a white-haired old man wearing a parson's collar.

My brother held out the parcel, and I was quite surprised to hear myself speak.

We found them, I said.

Did you now? the old man said, and he looked at me as he unwrapped the paper.

I found them, my brother said, and the old man looked at him.

We both found them, I said.

Well indeed now, did you both find them? the old man said, and he laughed as he put the beads in his pocket.

Would you boys like some lemonade? he said, and he told the fat lady to bring some, and then he leaned against the door-post and asked us what our names were. He certainly had a way with him and he soon had us talking.

My brother said he might be getting a bicycle for his birth-day, and I said he'd promised to let me ride it. This wasn't quite true, but I was hoping it might have some effect on my brother.

Then the fat lady brought the lemonade, with a straw in each glass, and when I'd finished I asked if I could keep the straw. My brother, who'd given his glass back, said I wasn't to, but the old man gave him his straw. Then he said, Goodbye boys, and remembering granpa we both began to run down the path.

But round the first bend we came to a standstill. Granpa was coming up the path. There was a look on his face we'd never seen before, and he had the buggy whip in his hand.

The Big Game

A. P. GASKELL

The football match at Carisbrook was over. Dusk was already falling, and during the last part of the game the flight of the ball and even the movements of the players had been hard to follow in the failing light. Now, looking across the field, I could see the crowd dimly massing around the gates. Here and there a small yellow flame flickered where a smoker was lighting up, and the whole crowd moved under a thin blue haze of tobacco-smoke. After all the cheering the place seemed very quiet, and from the street outside came the noise of cars starting up and whining off in low gear, and a tram screeching round the corner under the railway bridge. Overhead the sky was clear with a promise of frost. A few small boys ran with shrill cries under the goalposts; the rest of the field lay empty in the grey light, and the smell of mud came through the damp air. I shivered and glanced down at my steaming jersey.

'Well you'd better go and get changed,' said Betty. 'I don't want you to catch cold. You'll be playing Southern next Saturday now, won't you?'

'Yes,' I said. 'They were bound to win today. Beating Kai-korai puts us level with them.'

'Will you be too tired for the dance?'

'My old knee feels a bit sore but I'll ring you after tea. I must go and get changed now. So long.'

I trotted in under the stand. The lights were on, the unshaded bulbs threw a cheap yellow glare over the walls of the dressing-rooms, and up into the girders and struts above. My football boots clumped along the boards of the passageway. I stamped to get some of the mud off and pushed open the door chalked 'Varsity A'.

Inside the dressing-room there was a strong human smell of sweaty togs, muddy boots and warm bodies as the men came prancing back naked from the showers and stood on the seats drying themselves. The room was crowded. Togs and boots lay over the floor, clothes hung emptily from the pegs, and men were everywhere, shoving, jostling, reaching out their arms to dry themselves or climb into a shirt and taking up more room. Everyone was happy now that the strain was over, talking, yelling, singing, intent on their warmth and comfort and the clean feel of dry clothes. It was good to relax and know that we wouldn't have that feeling of before-the-game nervousness for another week. Next week it was going to be solid. The match against Southern was the Big Game.

'Shut that door,' roared Buck as I came in. 'Hello, it's Bennie. Did she think you played a nice game? Did she see my try? What did it look like from the stand?'

'They couldn't see it from the stand,' I said. 'They all thought you'd torn your pants when we gathered round you. Nobody knew it was a try.' I sat down and started picking at my muddy laces. My hands were too cold to grip them properly.

'Bloody liar,' said Buck amiably. 'It was a damn good try.' He had a very powerful voice. 'Boy oh boy oh boy,' he chanted, 'won't I knock back those handles tonight. You wait till I tell old Harry about my try. He'll shout after every round.'

'What try?' said Mac, our captain. 'Hell, you aren't going to claim anything for that bit of a scuffle? You were a mile offside.' His head disappeared into his shirt and came grinning out the top. He put on his glasses and the grin seemed more complete.

'Like hell,' shouted Buck, dancing about on the seat and sawing the towel across his back. 'I took the ball off him and fell over. When they all got off me there I was over the line. A clear try.'

'Offside a mile. Rabbiting. You handled it on the ground. I was walking back for the free-kick,' said the boys. They all liked Buck.

'Free-kick be damned,' he roared. 'It was a good forward's try. Right out of the book. Plenty of guts and initiative.'

'Yes, a typical forward's try,' said Bob, our half-back. He was small and very sturdy and freckled. 'Big bullocking bastards always mauling each other about. Why can't you do something nice and clean-cut like the backs?'

'The backs? The pansies? I sweat my guts out getting the ball

for you and then you canter along very prettily about ten yards
and then drop it.' He struck a chesty attitude standing naked
on the seat. 'Do I look like a pansy?'

'Not with that thing.'

Someone shied a ball at Buck and left a muddy mark on
his backside. I went out to the shower. I could hear Buck's
voice as I trotted along the passage. One of the Kaikorai men
was still in the shower-room.

'How are you now?' he said.

'Pretty tired. It was a tough game.'

'We didn't want you to have it too easy. You jokers will be
playing off with Southern now.'

'Yes. The big championship. Next Saturday.'

'Think you'll lick them?'

'Hope so. We'll give them a good go, especially if it's a dry
ground.'

'Their forwards are good. Pack very low. Well, good luck.'

'Thanks.' I turned on the taps. There was still plenty of hot
water left and it was great. Gosh I enjoyed it.

When I got back most of the boys were dressed and the
coach was there talking to Mac. 'Shake it along Bennie,' said
Bob, 'or we'll miss the beer. It's well after five now.'

'I'm practically there already,' I said. 'Don't rush me. Give
me a smoke. Hell I feel good now.' I was in digs with Bob.
'What did the coach think of it?'

'He said you were lousy but the rest of us went well.'

I knew Bob was joking but I didn't like it much. I knew I
wasn't particularly good and the coach was always on to me to
put more vigour and initiative into my play. I was the heaviest
man in the team and he would point out what the lighter
forwards did and then what I did, and make me feel ashamed.
If he thought I was lousy that meant I was in for a roasting at
the next team-talk.

'He says you're to mark Jackie Hore on Saturday,' grinned
Bob. 'You've got to dominate him.'

'I can easy fix Yackie,' I said. 'I bumped into him one game
last season and he fell over. Fell right over from just a little
bump. He's a softie.'

'Yes? Who was it broke your nose?'

'Aw, that was just his knee. Everybody's got hard knees.' I
struggled into my shirt.

'Listen! Listen!' Mac was yelling about the din. After the
uproar the silence sounded immense.

'Well boys,' said the coach. 'You know you're for it now. It's either you or the Southern for this season's champions, and next Saturday you'll have the honour of playing off with them. It's up to every one of you to keep fit. It's going to be a long hard game and I know I can rely on you boys to go on the field fit. I know Buck will leave the beer alone tonight.'

'What,' roared Buck, 'why do you think I go tearing round there for ninety minutes if it's not to get a thirst?'

'I knew you wouldn't mind,' said the coach, 'especially after they presented you with that try.'

'Another one,' said Buck in mock resignation. 'Another one. The best forward on the ground and I get nothing but abuse, I'll chuck the game and take on ping-pong.'

'Well boys, I'll see you on Wednesday at practice. I want you all out early. Will they all be out, Mac?'

'Anyone who can't?' said Mac. No answer.

'O.K. then. Goodnight boys. Anyone coming my way?'

They all began drifting off. Mac waited on Bob and me. The Southern match was just a nice distance ahead. I could get a thrill out of thinking of it but no nervousness yet. I felt good.

'Well Mac,' I said, 'how does the skipper feel about our chances? Our great public would like to know. Would you care to make a statement?' We often did these cross-talk acts.

'I think I may say with all due modesty that we are quietly confident,' said Mac. 'Tell our public that the same spirit of healthy rivalry that has spurred on our predecessors will again be found animating the bosoms of this year's team. Tell them that the game of Rugby fosters the team spirit and is the basis of our democracy. Tell them to play up and play the game. Tell them to go to hell.'

'Very prettily put,' I said. 'And now who else can we help?'

'A message for the expectant mothers,' urged Bob.

Mac was going well. 'Tell them we favour the quick heel,' he said. 'Never leave an opening for your opponent. God save Sir Truby King. For Christ's sake hurry up Bennie.'

I was dumping my togs in the bag as the caretaker put his head round the door. 'You boys ready? I'm waiting to lock up.'

We went out with him. 'Think you can hold the Southern?' he asked. He called them 'Southeren'.

'We'll give them a good go for it,' said Mac. He was our spokesman on occasions like these.

'They've got a fine team. You'll need all your luck to beat those forwards of theirs—man!'

'We're going to play fifteen backs and run them off the paddock,' said Bob.

'Are you now? Ay? Well I'll be watching you, but I'll no say which side I'll be barracking for. Goodnight.' He locked the gate after us.

It was quite dark now and all the street-lights were on. The air was keen and frosty. We went up under the railway bridge and stood in front of the lighted shops waiting for a tram. I was beginning to feel cold and stiff and tired now that the excitement was over.

'You know,' I said, 'football would be a good game if we could just play it on a Saturday.'

'Come up to date boy,' said Bob. 'This is Saturday. You remember yesterday? Well that was Friday. Today we've just beaten Kaikorai.'

'I bet he carries a calendar,' grinned Mac to me.

'No, fair go,' said Bob seriously. 'It's just general knowledge.'

'I mean it,' I said. 'It would be good if we could just play it on a Saturday. I've just been thinking, here we are just after slogging through one hard game and before we're off the ground even, everyone wants to play next week's game with us. Why can't they give us a spell?'

'I suppose they're greedy,' said Mac. 'They just get over one sensation and they're greedy for the next. They don't like having nothing to look forward to.'

'Hero worship too,' said Bob. 'They like to air their views in front of the well-known Varsity skipper. It makes them feel big. Or perhaps they think we don't bother about much else, we just live for football.'

'We will be for the next week,' I said. 'We'll be playing Southern all week and by the time Saturday comes we'll be so nervous we can't eat. It's one hell of a caper in a way. I'll be glad when the season's over and I can relax.'

'Did you get any knocks?'

'No worse than usual. The knee's pretty sore.'

The tram came along. It was good to sit down again. The conductor evidently recognised Mac. 'They'll make you run around next week,' he said. 'The Southern I mean. Be a good game.'

'How did they get on today?'

'Against Taieri? 46-3,' he said. 'How do you feel now?' He laughed and went to the back of the car. He came past us again later. '46-3,' he said again and winked.

The next Saturday morning I woke early in the digs and looked out the window. The sky was right down on the hills and there was a thick drizzle. O hell. I stretched down under the blankets again and tried to go to sleep but the thought of the match kept me awake. It had been a tough week as we were getting close to exams and I'd had a good deal of swot to do but I felt very fit. We'd been for a run every night after finishing our swot, usually about midnight, and on Wednesday there had been a really hard practice. The coach kept us packing lower and lower, scrum after scrum, and kept us down there with the strain on for so long that my muscles were all quivering and Buck who locked with me was groaning under the pressure, and when we stood up I felt dizzy and queer little lights slid down across my vision. It felt a good scrum though, very compact. The line-outs afterwards were plain hell. And then of course, the team-talk on Friday night. We used to hold it in a lecture room in the School of Mines. All around us on the wall were wooden models of pieces of machinery and charts of mines and geological strata. They made you realise the earth is very big and old, and goes down a long way. The coach would stand on the platform and start on his old game of building us up to fighting pitch. He was an artist at it, he could mould us just the way he wanted us. He spoke for a while about the traditions of the Club and then about the honour of playing off for the championship. 'Tomorrow,' he said, 'we'll start off as usual by taking them on in the forwards. Here I am in the line-out. I look at my opposite number and I think, "You're a good man, but by Jesus I'm a better. Today you've got no show".' His voice takes on a stirring note. He moves about on the platform suiting actions to his words. 'Into them! Dominate them! And every man when he sees where that ball goes, he thinks, "There's Buck in. I'm in too." Into them! And every man is thinking the same and we're all animated with the same spirit, we're going in to dominate them and we pack in tight and we're giving all our weight and strength and we're thinking together and working together and no one lets up. Dominate them.' And he goes on acting the part, words pouring out of him in that stirring tone and we watch him mesmerised, so that he takes us with him and we're there in the game, too, playing with him, working as a team. We leave the lecture room with a feeling of exaltation.

Then, on the other hand, there were the football notes in the paper. I know it was silly to take much notice of them, but I always read them. Referring to the Kaikorai game, the reporter said that I 'went a solid game but lacked the fire and dash that would make all the difference to his play'. The best thing I'd done, the movement where, to my mind, I had shown fire and dash was credited to Buck as 'one of his typical dashes'. Of course we are very much alike in build, but all the same I felt disappointed. The papers make people think that we are a sort of entertainment troupe, a public possession. Actually, I suppose we'd go on playing if there were no public; we'd relax and enjoy our football much more.

It's one hell of a caper really, I thought, stretching out under the sheets. I was lucky to have a girl like Betty who was keen on football. Some of the girls used to go very snooty when the blokes couldn't take them to the Friday night hops.

Well, this is the day. A few hours and it will be all over. This is it. It's funny how time comes round. For ages you talk of something and think of it and prepare for it, and it's still a long way off. You keep thinking how good it will be, and then suddenly, bang, it's there, you're doing it and it's not so enjoyable after all. I think football's like that, better before and after the game than in it.

Well, the day had come. I wasn't keen to get up and face it but anything was better than lying in bed and thinking a lot of rubbish. I put on dressing-gown and slippers and padded round to Bob's room. He was still asleep. 'You won't look so peaceful in eight hours time,' I said. 'They're queueing up at Carisbrook already.'

He raised his head from the pillow with a start. 'Eh?' He rubbed his eyes. 'What's wrong?'

'Jackie Hore just rang up to see how you are. He said their forwards are going to break very fast today, so he probably won't have an opportunity to ask you after the game because you'll be in hospital.'

He grinned. 'Then it's all bluff? I thought it was.'

'What?'

'About you forwards dominating them. I didn't think you could. I've never seen you do it yet. Just a bunch of big good-natured guys.'

'Not us,' I said. 'A pack of wolves just a-howling for prey. That's how we'll be today.'

Bob yawned and stretched his arms above his head. 'I must watch you. It would be interesting for a change. Have you eaten yet?'

So we went down for breakfast. Afterwards I cleaned my footy boots and packed my gear, and there was nothing to do but wait. I had no lectures on Saturday morning and I couldn't settle down to swot. The weather began to clear and a watery sun showed through the clouds so Bob and I went for a stroll. The town would be full of football talk and trams placarded, 'Big Game Today, Carisbrook 3 p.m., Varsity A v. Southern', so to get away from it we went down to Logan Park and climbed up above the quarry. It wasn't so cold in the sun and the harbour looked glassy. There was no-one about. We threw stones down into the quarry. It was good watching them. They dropped away from us, slowly getting smaller and smaller, then suddenly they struck the bottom and exploded shooting fragments out sideways, starlike.

At twelve we went back to the digs for an early lunch. I didn't feel very hungry, and while we were waiting for the food, Bob kept tapping with his knife on the table. We caught the quarter past one tram out to the ground. It was better to watch the curtain-raiser than hang about the digs. The tram was packed and rows of cars were already making for the ground. Everybody looked very jolly and expectant. We saw Buck and Mac on the tram and that cheered us up a bit. It was good to realise that there were others who had to go through with it too. Buck didn't care a hoot about it all.

'Think you can win?' an old man said to him.

'Win?' Buck seized the old fellow's hand. 'Be the first to congratulate us on winning the championship. Get in early. Do it now. Be the very first.'

The old chap pulled his hand away looking a bit silly.

At Carisbrook we joined the crowd around the gates and pushed through to the players' entrance. I could see people nudging one another and nodding towards Mac. We showed our passes and went in along behind the stand and in underneath to the dressing-rooms. Most of the boys were early, there were other bags lying on the seats.

'Shall we go up for a while?' said Mac. We went out in front of the stand to see the final of the Junior Competition. The stand was packed and the bank opposite was dark with people. We stood about watching the boys playing with a sort of detached interest and then at half-time we went underneath to change. The strain was getting to me a little—I'd take things off and then forget where I'd put them. I had to undo my pants and look to see whether I'd put on my jockstrap. Most of the chaps were pretty quiet, but Buck kept going and we were pleased we had him to listen to. Mac was roaming round in his underpants looking for his glasses.

'Like to make a statement before the match?' I asked him.

He just looked at me. 'I can't find my bloody glasses. I suppose some bastard will tread on them.'

'Just a picture of quiet confidence,' said Bob. My face felt very tight when I tried to grin.

Soon the trainer came in and started to rub us down. The room was filled with the smell of eucalyptus and the rapid slap slap slap of his hands. It was a great feeling being done, he made us feel nice and loose and warm and free-moving. Then Jackie Hore, the Southern skipper, came in to toss and we looked at him. There he was, the man we had been talking about all the week. He lost the toss and laughed. He looked a good deal smaller than I'd been imagining him. Of course we had played against him before, but the strain makes you think silly things. We felt better after he'd gone.

'He doesn't look so soft,' said Bob to me.

'Poor old Yackie. I'll try and bump into him again today and you just watch.'

'Never mind,' he said, 'unless you do it from the other side and straighten your nose up.'

I strapped up my weak knee and when the vaseline came round plastered it on my face to prevent scratches. The coach came in and we packed a scrum for him.

'That looks all right,' he said. 'Well now, listen boys. Remember you're going out now as the Varsity boys have done for many years now to play off for the championship, and a lot of those old players are out there today watching to see how good you are. Don't let them down. Remember the first ten minutes in the forwards. Hard!' He punched his open hand. 'Go in there and dominate . . . .' But the referee was in the room to inspect the boots and the coach's exhortation was lost in the movement.

'Righto boys. One minute to go,' said the ref.

We took off our coats and handed round chewing gum. Buck and I put on our ear-guards. Mac found the ball and we lined up in the passage. The Southern players were there already, skipping about and rubbing their hands. They felt the cold too. The whistle blew, there was a glare of sunlight, and we were outside going out into the field, right out into the open. A roar from the crowd rolled all around enveloping us. A cold easterly breeze blew through our jerseys as we lined up for the photographers, squinting into the low sun. The Southern players looked broad and compact in their black and white jerseys. We gave three cheers and trotted out into the middle. The turf felt fine and springy. We spaced ourselves out. I took some deep breaths to get charged up with oxygen for this first ten minutes. A Southern player dug a hole with his heel and placed the ball.

'All right Southern? All right Varsity?' called the referee. Both captains nodded. He blew the whistle. The Southern man ran up to kick.

'Thank Christ,' I thought. 'The game at last.'

The Everlasting Miracle

RODERICK FINLAYSON

At Tidal Creek there was a young Maori called Monday Wiremu. Like most of the other boys of his gang, Monday was a hard case. He worked no more than he could help. He spent his time, and the other fellow's money, gambling and drinking. 'Eh, goody-goody all right for the Pakeha,' said Monday. 'This Maori boy means to have a good time.'

Monday had a girl over Wainui way. Maggie Peka was her name. He was rather off-hand about her. She didn't get much of his money. He fancied it smart to treat the women rough, as he put it.

Young Monday Wiremu was a hard case, and folk said he would live and die the same.

Then, one night, he met the devil. That's what he said. The boys said he was drunk or he wouldn't have gone home alone late at night past the old boneyard.

Monday said his horse shied at something and threw him on his head. And there was old Nick all right. Old Nick said to him, 'Monday Wiremu, you get to hell out of this kind of thing. Monday, you go pray to God and do folk good. Don't you forget Monday Wiremu.'

Think what you like; Monday Wiremu was a changed man after that adventure. The sight of strong drink turned him sick. He said he hardly knew one card from another, and he couldn't remember the name of one racehorse. He just yawned at the mention of such things. He didn't go with the gang any more. The boys laughed at him. They strutted behind him singing, 'Holy, holy Monday!' But it was no use. He didn't seem to mind.

Worst of all, he wouldn't go to see his sweetheart, Maggie

Peka, out at Wainui any more. He said he was too busy trying to do good and heal the sick. He said you can't do good and cure the sick and run after women. Well, he cured Turi's cough, and he did his best for Hemi's old brindle cow that had the cough too.

'That old cow is more grateful than a woman,' said Monday.

All this became a bit of a nuisance for Tupara, the local tohunga, that old cure-all and fortune-teller. One day when Hoppy Crummer saw Tupara going by on his piebald nag he asked him what he thought of it.

'Hullo, Two-barrel,' he said. 'How do you like young Monday doing all your doctoring for you?'

'You see here, Hoppy,' said Tupara. 'Monday don't know a damn thing. Go round saying Jesus love you. Where the money come from, eh?'

And he went off lamming the old piebald with a willow stick.

'You wait. I fix him,' he shouted over his shoulder.

'Ha, ha!' laughed Hoppy Crummer. 'If the Parson was honest I guess he could say the same. He don't get much Maori cash in his collection plate now. All the Maoris are hot and strong for Monday. The new prophet they call him.'

Monday Wiremu said perhaps the scoffers would open their eyes wide when he walked on the water. Monday said he would walk on the water just to show all those people. He fixed it for next Sunday at the Rapids. He chose the Rapids because he had such a lot of faith. 'Peter the fisherman walked on a mighty big storm,' said Monday. 'So I walk across the Rapids.'

The Rapids were where the tide ripped around a headland on the upper reaches of Tidal Creek. Even a good swimmer might drown there. Monday couldn't swim. It seems that he was brought up by an aunt somewhere away inland.

This news upset the Parson. He said that people couldn't let a young man drown himself, and that it would be a great sin if someone else got drowned trying to save Monday. He said that he would preach against miracles next Sunday.

The boys of Monday's old gang, though, seemed to take the affair differently from what you would have expected. They hardly ever made a joke of Monday now. They almost wanted to help him in a sheepish sort of way. They didn't like the Pakehas slinging off about Maori prophets.

'The Pakeha haven't got one damn prophet,' they said. 'The Pakeha keep all the prophet packed away in the Bible and he don't like it when the Maori have the real live prophet that come out in the open and do the proper miracle in front of everyone's eyes, eh?'

Monday took no notice of anyone. He went about quietly and happily. When he met any of the boys at the store he said ordinary things like, 'How your uncle?' or 'How the ginger-pop today?'

On Sunday morning people began to gather on the beach above the Rapids. By mid-morning there was a big crowd there, so many in fact that it was difficult at first to find Monday Wiremu. Monday stood with a few friends away from the crowd under a clump of cabbage trees. It gave you a bit of a shock to see him dressed so gaily. It made you think of the seriousness of the occasion. Monday wore his cream tennis trousers, with a green blazer and his panama hat. He had a pink carnation in his button-hole, and he wiped his face with a large red silk handkerchief.

The people on the beach didn't take much notice of him. They made a picnic of it. You would have thought that walking on the waves was an everyday event. Everywhere you looked there were squalling kiddies and goory dogs and grey-headed old men with carved pipes and carved walking-sticks. There were fat women in white blouses and black skirts or red skirts or blue skirts, with scarves over their heads. There were wagon-ettes, and buggies and drays, and horses of all kinds hitched to cabbage trees. Some families were perched in the empty-shafted wagons or buggies in order to have a better view. The flash boys and the pretty girls strolled past each other on the beach, in groups, going in opposite directions.

The place buzzed with gossip. Tui Tinopai said that the Parson had sent for Constable Morris to come and stop what he called 'this blasphemy'. Tui said Constable Morris couldn't find anything dealing with miracles in the Police Regulations and he didn't want to make a fool of himself. So he was watching the proceedings through field-glasses from the top of the cliffs near the pub, said Tui.

And Ripi said that the school-kids were boasting about old Tupara putting a makutu curse on Monday. They saw red fires flickering around his place all night. They kept well away. It's good-bye and no God-bless-you if you get on the wrong side of a tohunga.

Ripi said that Tupara had just sent Hoho, the half-wit, peddling like mad on a bike he pinched from outside the church.

Hoho disappeared in the direction of Wainui. That was where Maggie Peka lived.

Mrs Tamahana wondered what Maggie Peka thought of Monday giving her the good-bye for this sideshow sort of business.

Presently Monday and his friends came down to the edge of the water and looked out over the swift-running tide. It looked a dreadful stretch of water to try to walk upon. The tide, rushing out, swept around the foot of a sheer rocky headland. You could see the whirlpools and the choppy places and the currents that sucked under the rocky ledges. The whole place seemed dark and terrible and not at all like the sunny, open waters of the bay.

Monday prayed. That quietened the gossipy buzz and focused all attention on Monday. Then he spoke to the people about Peter the fisherman who walked on the waves, and about miracles, and how everyone soon would have faith to believe. Monday's face shone and he spoke so feelingly that you were sure that God would give such a man power to do anything. Everyone was carried away by Monday's eloquence.

After that it all seemed to happen in a few winks of the eye. There was a scraggy pohutukawa tree leaning out over the waves at the beginning of the bluff, hanging on to the cliff by a few twisty old roots. Monday walked to this tree, took hold of the overhanging branch and lowered himself down to the swirling water till his feet just about touched its surface. His band of followers gathered around singing a triumphant sort of hymn.

It looked very funny at first to see Monday in his best clothes, with his panama hat and his button-hole, letting himself down into the sea. Then you listened to the singing and you remembered that he was going to walk *on* the water, not fall *into* the water. It made all the difference.

Some swear that they saw Monday walk on the water. Perhaps they were right. Things like miracles happen quickly, and you're not used to seeing such extraordinary events.

But as the singing ended, in the middle of the breathless hush as Monday poised himself on the tops of the waves just getting his shoes wet, there was a commotion at the back of the crowd. Men and women and children jumped hastily aside, and Maggie Peka pedalled furiously into the group on the Parson's bike. She jumped from the machine, and it took two or three women to stop her from throwing herself over the cliff.

Hearing the commotion, Monday looked up. He took a long,

long look. Every detail of that scene must have printed itself deep in his memory—the girl in her old blue dress: among all the finery of the others she was bare-legged and hatless in an old faded dress. Her hair blew wildly in the wind, her strong legs and arms and her whole body strained to break away from the women, to leap into the sea to be with Monday. What her eyes were like only Monday could tell. He looked straight into her eyes.

Monday Wiremu had just let go of the tree, and lots of people swore that he was walking on the water. But after that one long look at Maggie he seemed to shrug his shoulders and fall right through the water. He sank like a stone.

Women screamed and men shouted advice to one another. Children began to cry and dogs to howl. People rushed here and there. All was confusion.

But scarcely had Monday gone under the water and bobbed up again than a boat, manned by some of the boys of the gang, shot out from the shelter of the headland, where it had been waiting for this very moment, and fished Monday out of the sea.

After that everyone was emphatic that Monday had walked on the water. If it hadn't been for that Maggie Peka hussy he would have walked right to the other side, they all agreed. They couldn't do enough for Monday. They wanted to build him a meeting-house where he could preach and cure the sick.

The funny thing, though, was that Monday didn't want to be thought a prophet after that.

'No,' he insisted, 'no good to call me the prophet. Monday Wiremu not the good saint, just the poor bad man.'

What he *did* want was to marry Maggie Peka. And he married her.

'That the miracle,' he tells his friends. 'How a man want to put up with a girl like this all his life—that the miracle, eh? That the everlasting miracle.'

Old Tupara, who listens at a distance, just winks.

Showers

FRANK SARGESON

This big fellow got the name of Showers, because he would never answer anything else whenever he was asked what the weather was going to be. Also he worked for the town board, and in the dry weather he'd have to drive about the streets on the water-cart, and that sort of fitted in with his nickname as well.

Anyhow, Showers was a man who was said to weigh just on twenty stone, and as he wasn't specially tall you can imagine what he looked like. He was a good sort though, everybody liked him with his big red face that was always breaking into a grin, and he never seemed to mind when you pulled his leg by asking him what the weather was going to be.

Showers lived with his mother, just the two of them living in a small house, and there were all sorts of yarns about the size of his appetite, and the quantity of meat his mother was always buying. The butcher, having his drinks along at the pub, would say how it was nothing unusual for Showers' mother to buy half a fair-sized sheep on Saturday, and then be back again on Monday morning wanting another half. But everybody always said the butcher was exaggerating, because it might take a lot to feed Showers, but not as much as all that. The butcher would say no, it was the fair dinkum truth, and he'd get annoyed when he couldn't get anyone to believe him. And then one day he told an even better one. He said that one Friday late shopping night Showers' mother had bought a whole calf and had it delivered early Saturday morning, and on Sunday morning early she was round at the butcher's house asking him please would he get something for her out of the shop, because she was right out of meat.

But there was nobody along at the pub at the time who would swallow that one, and the butcher got very annoyed, and it led to a lot of argument. A cow-cocky who was reckoned to be pretty well in said he'd killed and eaten a lot of meat in his time, and he knew for a fact that no man, not even with the help of his old mother, could eat a whole calf in practically one day. So the butcher said all right, was he prepared to bet on it? And after a lot of talk it was all fixed up. The bet was to be a tenner, and Showers was to eat a whole calf, bones not included of course, between sunrise and sunset on anniversary day. The way they fixed it was like this: the day before the holiday the butcher was to deliver the calf to the pub-keeper, and he was to get the cook to make the meat into patties, and all the holiday a plateful of them was to be kept on the bar counter, and nobody was to take anything from that plate except Showers; though it was decided Showers wasn't to be in the know, and nobody was to let on to him, but there'd be no trouble because he was fond of his beer, and if he was stood enough drinks it was reckoned he'd stay in the pub long enough to give the calf a fair go.

So everything was fixed up, and on anniversary day, sure enough, Showers came along to the pub soon after it opened up in the morning. Of course the news about the bet had got around, and there were quite a few side-bets on the go as well, so quite a crowd was there to see if Showers would fall down on the job. But he didn't show any signs of it all through the morning, though just before midday the cow-cocky took the butcher by the sleeve and led him round into the kitchen, and people said the butcher came back pulling a long face. And others went to look and came back winking at their cobbers, and said he'd never do it, because he hadn't finished off nearly half a great big trayful so far, and there was another big one still to go.

Though it wasn't long before things began to look up for the butcher, because Showers let himself be persuaded that, seeing it was a holiday, he might as well make a day of it and cut out going home for his dinner. And once having made the decision he whacked into the patties a good deal faster, though his backers weren't any too pleased when, instead of sticking to the patties, he'd once or twice reach out for a piece of bread and cheese off one of the other plates.

Then he slackened off again, which after all was hardly anything more than was natural, but his backers got windy when he said maybe he'd better be going home for a snooze now, because later on he wanted to do a bit of work in the garden. But he couldn't resist having another few drinks first, and he'd eat a patty now and then, though sometimes he'd nearly break a number of hearts by taking one up while he talked—but only to put it back on the plate again. Later on though he began to get hungry again, and when it was getting on towards evening and the pubkeeper said free drinks all round, and let everybody eat up too—well, Showers just went right ahead. And packed to the doors though the bar was, you could have heard a pin drop when he took the last patty on the plate, and everybody knew there wasn't a single one more to come.

Of course the next moment there would have been wild cheers and a great hullabaloo, but some wag picked up a plate with one last piece of bread and cheese and held it out to Showers. And he didn't speak very clearly (after all, besides the patties, he'd put away quite as much beer as was good for him), but he was understood to say no thanks, he didn't think he ought to, because he'd heard a yarn about somebody having a bet on to get him to eat a whole calf before sundown.

Yes, to the Very End

'AUGUSTUS' (R. A. COPLAND)

The service-car pulled out of Gisborne just as the sun was pulling in. We were a cold and melancholy lot, packed in rows down the car as in theatre seats without arms. One or two faces, wanner than the rest, had grown familiar to me during innumerable excursions to railway refreshment rooms the day before. The pies, sandwiches and tea from Paekakariki to Wairoa were still compressed and uneasy behind those faces.

The driver looked neat and fresh and efficient. He made me feel old.

The back seat was hilariously occupied by four Maori youths, whose provisions for the journey were some crayfish and a guitar. Soon the emanations of both were floating along the low ceiling. A hundred and fifty miles were certainly no hardship to those lads, and at the finish it was the others who were staring gaunt, glazed and emaciated upon the land of the long white cloud.

We left the flat country pretty soon and the driver began the long wrestle with the gear-lever which, from then on, was seldom out of his hand. All the way he maintained the utmost speed which the weight of his cargo and the precipitousness of the terrain would allow him. He swept round curves, plunged down chasms, hurtled over one-way bridges and surged up slopes with uniform indifference, and only the sweat of the engine whose fumes drifted back and mingled with the crayfish and the *Ferry-boat Serenade* betrayed the ardours of our progress.

The road was monotonously hair-raising. Its builders had shown a perverse predilection for the cliff-and-abyss style, declining always to saunter along the bottom of valleys, and blasting a track into the near-vertical sides of the grimmest mountains they could find.

Nature had done her best to soften the prospect, and the menace of gravity was everywhere glossed over with glistening dark-green bush. One felt that when the bus did plunge over the edge at the next bend the descent would be noiseless and comfortable into the torrent hundreds of feet below.

The road was just wide enough for our bus, and every now and then we would roar past a sheep truck coming in the opposite direction. The driver would wave an airy hand.

Once a red and yellow notice board edged into the roadway and had the effrontery to suggest that as a slip had occurred on the road ahead, a certain amount of caution might be exercised. The bus sneered past the notice, no paint apparently being removed from either. The slip had gnawed a semi-circle back into the road, but the bus had sufficient speed to clear it. From my window I glanced down for a second into eternity.

Then an old hand behind the driver noticed a bush away on the other side of the world which was all ablaze with scarlet. 'What's that Mac?' he asked the driver, and everyone looked sadly in the direction of his pointing arm, expecting a volcano or a dinosaur. The driver left off driving and studied the flaring patch. The bus changed its gears and swirled round a bend.

'Hanged if I know, George,' the driver admitted at last.

'Would it be rata?' the lady near me ventured to the paralysed passengers. We all took up the cue. The psychologists call it sublimation, I think. The pressure of terror becomes so great that you feign an interest in the trivial. We all became wildly speculative about the scarlet bush, and I rummaged through the remains of Nature Study, thankful that no one knew I was the new Rector of Wairenga-o-roaroa.

When we came to a Public Works camp the driver actually stopped the bus. A vast weight of accumulated speed piled up and oppressed us in the sudden and silent no-motion. Outside the camp a Maori stood with his hands in his pockets. He was big enough and preposterous enough to have built the road himself. He might have had a hand in landing Maui's fish. Just to look at him made the tale a shade less fabulous.

The driver asked him about the coloured bush. He suggested rata, and we all smiled knowingly and shook our heads at him. He wasn't in the least abashed. He thrust his trousers forwards from the pockets, shrugged his shoulders and beamed at us.

'Aw, the hell,' he roared, 'how would I know—I don't belong to this country.'

Pretty obviously the country belonged to him. He could have pushed the bus off the road if he'd taken his hands out of his pockets. So we started off again. Every now and then the driver would wind his window down slowly. Then he would grope under his seat, produce a newspaper, roll it tightly up with both hands, bend it, and having apparently completed these preliminaries at exactly the right spot on the road, he would hurl the paper over the roof of the bus.

I watched for the paper to descend on my side. It would plop into the grass by the roadside. There it lay, a white speck, brand new, tiny and isolated. For miles and miles on every side the land was twisted and heaved into ranges and hills, valleys and gullies, a gigantic rubble heap which centuries had flimsily covered with grass and bush. There was not a sign of human habitation anywhere. I tried to believe that somewhere, tucked into a hillside there was a house. Someone in the house would come to find that paper every day, and so keep up a kinship with us in the bus, and with Mr Truman and with Princess Elizabeth.

At one stage the bus slowed down and stopped. Only the driver and one passenger knew why. There was nothing on the road, no sign-board, no gate, no mail-box—just a place on the road and a place on the map distinguished no more than that it had a latitude and longitude.

A large woman scrambled out on to the shingle. The driver produced a suitcase from somewhere that clanged at the back, and handed it to the woman. She sat down on the bag, solid, capable and expressionless. Someone would be coming to meet her, knowing exactly where to find her. Perhaps she had been staying for a fortnight with her married sister in town, making beds, washing dishes, peeling potatoes—she would be home in time for the milking if they remembered to call for her; if they found her all right.

I looked at the immense earth and the unbroken sky, at a frail fence groping away down the slope, charred and broken tree-stumps puncturing the cleared ground. And I looked at the woman sitting there placid and strong. She'd be called for, I decided. In any case, she'd get home.

The township when we arrived looked somehow gauche and

innocent. We pressed into it, bringing as it were the bridled impetus of a hundred and fifty miles. We brought dust and heat and experience compacted into a solid wedge of steel, rubber, glass and human enterprise. We deferred to the township by courtesy. We were too far gone for the township to have stopped us. The people in the streets were too young.

As I was leaving the bare and petrol-reeking barn of a garage I said, 'So long' to the driver. 'Well, that was an experience,' I said, trying to pretend those giddy feet were my own.

'That the first time you've travelled by service-car?' he asked.

'Oh, no, not really. I used to go by bus quite a lot between Timaru and Christchurch.'

He smiled politely like the big-game hunter whose host was telling about the time the canary got out.

A Small Story (for F. S.)

MAURICE DUGGAN

The fairhaired boy and the fairhaired girl swung on the gate. They stood with their feet thrust between the wooden rungs and pushed the gate back and rode on it as it swung forward. They had been forbidden to ride on the gate but that was another time; each day had its own rules.

The sun shone. The dust on the pavement stirred.

They were waiting for the postman.

The concrete road that ran past the house shimmered in the heat. On the opposite side of the street a gate like the one on which they swung had written on it, Sans Souci. No Hawkers. For the boy and the girl it was an exotic name. They did not puzzle over it. Their own gate had no name. There was a number on the gatepost.

The postman cycled along the footpath. He stopped at the gate.

—We're a bit late today, he said. He was sweating.

The girl took the letters. The postman said Goodbye, and don't go loosing them, and rode off. He bumped his pushbike across the kerb and crossed the road to Sans Souci.

The girl looked at the letters. The letter on top was addressed to Mrs Lenihan.

—It's to Missus Lenihan, she told the boy.

His long face smiled at her.

—That was mother's name, the girl said.

The boy pushed back the gate and let it go. It swung forward and banged shut.

—Whee, the boy said.

—People don't write to dead people, the girl said.

A sparrow flew into the hedge. They heard the noise it made

but could not see it. A bus went by on the road and they both waved. The girl waved the letter. The bus windows winked back.

—Is Dad coming? the boy asked.

—Not till next week, the girl said.

—Is the maid coming? he asked.

—You shouldn't call her the maid. Call her Aunt Grace.

—Is she coming?

—I don't know, the girl said. Perhaps next week.

The boy got the gate back and gave a push with his foot and it slammed shut and they both jumped off.

—You hurt my stomach, the girl said.

The boy looked at her.

—They're married, the girl said. I knew it all the time. I guessed it when they went away. She's Missus Lenihan.

—Who is?

—Who do you think? Aunt Grace, of course.

—Are they coming back? the boy asked.

—I don't know, the girl said.

She climbed on to the gate. She began to swing it on her own.

—You're too rough, she said. They might be gone for good.

They ran through the house to the front door and when they opened it there was their father standing there. They had seen his shadow through the glass panel. He picked them up, one on each arm, and kissed them, the girl first then the boy. Over his shoulder they saw a taxi in the road and the driver mounting the steps carrying a suitcase in each hand.

—Put them anywhere, Mr Lenihan said, putting the boy and the girl down. Uh, you're ton weights. What's the damage? he asked the driver.

He rattled the change in his pocket and put two coins in the driver's hand. The driver looked at it.

—That's right, the driver said, and went down the steps.

Mrs Lenihan was on her way up.

—It's a stiff climb, the driver said to the new Mrs Lenhian.

Mr and Mrs Lenihan and the boy and the girl went into the house. Mr Lenihan put the bags down outside the bedroom door.

—Hadn't we better tell them and get it over? Mrs Lenihan said.

—Perhaps we'd better, Mr Lenihan said.

The children followed them into the large bedroom. The blinds were pulled down in an even row over three-quarters the length of each window. The sun shone through small pin-sized holes in the blind. The curtain flared in the draught. On the dark polished table the cut glass bottles of a toilet set were spaced out on lacework mats.

Mrs Lenihan unpinned her hat before the mirror and ran her hands through her hair. She sat on the edge of the bed. In the bed's centre, flounced, sat a kewpie doll.

—I can't use her things, Mrs Lenihan said to her husband. She nodded at the cut glass bottles.

—Just as you like, Mr Lenihan said.

—Well, can I? Mrs Lenihan said.

—No, I suppose not, Mr Lenihan said. We'll put them out of the way somewhere. But now . . . and his eyes slipped to the children.

They stood just inside the door. Mrs Lenihan held out her hands to them, and smiled.

—I've got a surprise for you, Mr Lenihan said.

He had rehearsed the next sentence all the way back from the train, in the taxi, and now it failed him. After all, I've no idea how they see things, he had said to his wife. And, Oh bosh! Mrs Lenihan had abruptly said.

—This is your new mother, Mr Lenihan said.

Mrs Lenihan widened her smile. Her great bosom swelled, her rouge flushed face went darker; her blue eyes, protruding, blinked. She was animated with fond feelings.

The children looked and looked.

—We'll have to decide what you're to call your mother, Mr Lenihan said. Is it to be mother or mum or mummy, or what? I'm not too keen on mummy, he said. But whatever you think.

—Grace, the girl said.

—Grace, the boy echoed.

—That won't do, Mr Lenihan said. She's not Aunt Grace any more, you know that. She's your mother now. Can't you call her mother?

—That's right, don't mind me, Mrs Lenihan said. Just make out I'm not here.

—I'm sorry, dear, Mr Lenihan said. He patted her shoulder.

—We called our mother, mother, the girl said.

Mr and Mrs Lenihan looked briefly at one another and seemed in unison, impatiently, to sigh.

—What do you say, young Harry? Mr Lenihan said.

—I don't know, the boy said.

—Why won't Aunt Grace do? the girl said.

—We'll call you the maid, the boy said.

—You will not, Mrs Lenihan said. For that's what I'm not. I'm not to be your maid, and that's clear. I hope you can all get that into your head. I'm to be nobody's maid. I suppose Miss Margaret put you up to that one.

—I did not, the girl said. And I'm not Miss Margaret, I'm Margaret.

Mrs Lenihan stirred on the bed and stood up. She had kicked off her shoes. She thudded across to the children and stood over them. She smelled strongly of perfume and lightly of sweat. She wore an engagement ring and a wedding ring and on the other hand a ring with a red stone shone in the light.

—Come along, she said. After all you'll have to call me something, won't you now? Or what say you think about it? There's no hurry is there? Your father and I have a lot to do and you can come back and tell us later.

—That's the idea, Mr Lenihan said. Run along and think it over, and we'll come out and see you later on.

—Give us a kiss first, Mrs Lenihan said.

Harry, pushed forward by his father's hand, was folded to her sweet smelling laced bosom and firmly kissed. Margaret took her kiss on the crown of her head, through her fair hair. They went out of the room.

While the door closed, and while they were still near enough to hear, Mr Lenihan laughed. Margaret bent her head to the door and listened. Her hair fell forward over her eyes.

—You've taken on a handful there, Mr Lenihan said.

—Nonsense, Mrs Lenihan said. The boy will come round soon enough. I've always managed with boys.

They laughed together.

—Things are probably strange, Mr Lenihan said.

—Oh don't worry about them now, Mrs Lenihan said. We'll manage. And she held out to her new husband her great arms, looking just beyond him at the kewpie on the flounced bed.

—You just wait, Margaret said. You'll soon see what she's like. She'll do awful things to you just to get her own way: and she'll shut you in your room in the dark, you see. She'll pinch you till you're black and blue. I heard her say.

—Did she pinch you? Harry said.

—Of course not, silly, Margaret said. She wouldn't dare.

—She smells nice, Harry said.

His sister caught him by the arm.

—Don't you say that again, she said. If you do I'll do something awful to you. I'll push you right under a bus. I will. She smells horrid. She's put mother's bottles away in a cupboard under the stairs. Mother never smelled like that. Don't you remember?

—I don't know, Harry said.

—You don't know anything, his sister said. I could give you a photo you could keep under your pillow, and you could look at it every night. Will you?

—What if they see? Harry said.

—They won't see, Margaret said. If they catch you looking you have to put it in your mouth and chew it up.

—Let's swing on the gate, Harry said.

—She'd stop us, Margaret said. You see. From now on we won't be allowed to do anything.

—Let's wait for the postman, Harry said.

—He's been, silly, Margaret said.

—What will we do then? Harry said.

—Nothing. Just nothing, Margaret said.

She opened the door and went down the steps to the front gate.

—Nothing, she said. If you promise to hate her, I'll tell you something. Do you promise? Promise, go on. Promise, Harry. Say I promise to hate her, all the time until we are both dead.

Harry stared at her. Her eyes were filling with tears. She was going to cry. He didn't understand.

—I promise, he said. Let's swing on the gate.

They opened the gate which had no name and climbed on to the lower rung and swung back and forth, back and forth, in complete silence.

Race Day

MAURICE DUGGAN

—Come on, Harry said.

—I've finished, Margaret said.

—Have you indeed? Mrs Lenihan said. And what's that on your plate?

—Get it down, there's a girl, Mr Lenihan said. It'll make your teeth curl and your hair white.

Margaret smiled, as at an old, old joke, and bent over her plate where the cooling porridge rose in mounds like tidal islands through the milk.

—Wait for your sister, Harry, Mr Lenihan said.

—I didn't hear anyone ask to leave the table, Mrs Lenihan said. But perhaps I'm going deaf.

—Say your piece, son, Mr Lenihan said.

—Just this once, Grace, Mr Lenihan said. They're itching to get out.

—They're itching, Mrs Lenihan said. And who are they?

—Off you go, Mr Lenihan said.

And they edged round the table and ran through the house, but not until they were wedged, side by side in a space between the verandah posts, did they begin to believe it was real, after all. But there it lay, a one-day wonder, an oval of rich green in the summer-coloured oblong park, washed on one side by the tide which rose through the mangroves and bound on the other by the shine of the harbour beach. Once each year they saw it as something wholly new. Their eyes looked out over the sunken houses and the road to where it lay, beyond and below, almost empty at this hour of the morning, but hung above with flags and rinsed in sun, a racecourse quite complete, for this one day in the year.

The sun warmed the wide rail on which they sat and the night's dew steamed still. Harry had his father's binoculars hung by their strap from his neck; as he leaned forward they knocked lightly on the wood. Below their dangling feet, a long way down, carnations tangled in the garden border.

The line of traffic thickened until it was a solid stream, moving slowly, turning down the side road under the signalling white-sleeved arms of a policeman on points duty. The cars rolled richly over the spurting gravel.

Mr and Mrs Lenihan crossed the wide verandah and began to descend the steps; Mrs Lenihan in purple and white—huge flowers like stains of dried blood on the silk—and Mr Lenihan in a grey suit that would, later in the day, be much too hot. A *Members' Enclosure* card hung from Mr Lenihan's lapel.

—What are you sitting on top of one another for? Mrs Lenihan asked. There's plenty of room.

—Be good kids, Mr Lenihan said. Remember to back all the outsiders and you can't go wrong.

They laughed and arm in arm climbed down.

Mr Lenihan blithely hummed:

> *Bet my money on a bobtail nag*
> *Somebody bet on the bay . . .*

—Goodbye, he called

And Harry put the binoculars wrong-end-round to his eyes and watched his father and his step-mother descend, small, precise and a long way off, a flight of steps that went down and down until they seemed to plunge like a spear into the lawn. He changed ends and they were at the gate, so out of focus that his eyes watered as if in grief, and his father's hand was waving right up against the glass. The binoculars made no difference to voices. He turned them end for end again and swept them around in a wide arc so that the earth seemed to spin past, from left to right, and Mr Toms, swinging on crutches three-legged though his garden, was appropriate denizen of a collapsing world.

—Please, Harry, let me look, Margaret said. Please. Before they are out of sight.

And she too turned the binoculars on those retreating backs and watched her father cross to the outside of the pavement and extend his doubled arm and, although it was all too far away for her to have heard anything, she knew her father would be saying, mocking: And if I might have the pleasure, Mrs Lenihan, in a brogue which, she did not know, he had preserved as carefully as the manner of his remarks in the years, a lifetime, since Dublin had seen him last. But had she known she would not have cared. What she saw was indistinguishable from what she felt and that brogue, telling tales, lay under her childhood like foundations of water. The tales seemed to whisper to her now from the magic glass.

And yet the grey back, turned solidly to her and moving away, mocked her too as she looked.

The racecourse, outside the oval of track, had lost to bright fashion its summer colour, and only inside the track, where a grey ambulance waited and a few men moved, was the grass still to be seen, brown and burned by the sun.

Margaret focused the glasses, won from Harry with promises she could never keep, until the whole racecourse lay, clear and close, almost under her hand. In the birdcage the horses for the first race circled and danced, perched on by jockeys as light and as perky and as gay as parakeets, and threaded out curving and sidestepping on to the unmarked track. Above the roofs of the buildings—the totalisator, the grandstand, the members' stand, the bar—the red balloon rode as no balloon ever rode, rigid at the mast, and away to the left the tide rose in patterns of light and shadow through the mangroves. The horses, rich as velvet, strained on tight reins past the grandstand, out to the barrier wires. Shredded by the breeze the tatters of music blew up, harsh and gay, to where the children sat, and with one arm hooked around the post Margaret stared through the binoculars.

—Can you see anything? Harry asked.

She did not answer.

Swinging and turning the horses came into line, broke, re-formed, and burst away, running in silence, charging, while the wide line narrowed and beat against the rails, and she saw them go into the bend and show again, smaller now, straining in the same amazing silence across the back straight, and run towards her, colour after colour bright in the sunlight, to come to the hurdles where, still in silence, they stretched out and hung a moment as though carved from something solid and eternally still, and ran on. They raced to a series of sounds—the banging of a gate, a radio playing, a car passing on the road—which served only to heighten the soundlessness within that charmed lens. She felt that she had by some magic entered a world where, because of that silence, nothing human might enter again; and even Harry, shouting for his turn, could not disturb it.

Slowly, in twos and threes, the horses rose and came on, fleeing across the confining circle until, when they were almost free, she shifted the binoculars and they were caught again. In the silence the billowing colours drummed and shone. She outpaced the running horses merely by moving her wrist and waited them at the double jump. The first horse rose to it and touched and rose again and was gone: the brush on the hurdle trembled. But before she too could swing away the following horses showered into the lens and, all grace gone, struck and fell, and a jockey in crimson and yellow silks and white breeches made an absurd clash of colour on the green grass.

Only when she took the binoculars from her eyes did the shouting beat up to her, blown, like the music, to shreds; whispering and roaring over the rooftops and the road.

—Could you see anything? Harry asked.

The air was growing cooler. A wind blew across the mangroves where now the tide had stolen from the muddy channels. They sat now out of their niche, on the top verandah step, and stared down: they had not spoken for a long time.

—How many have you got? Harry asked.

—I wasn't counting, Margaret said.

—I've got hundreds, Harry said. Not counting the people; they don't count.

—Not people, Margaret agreed.

—But horses do, and horse-floats do, Harry said. A horse-float is four and an ambulance is three—but I haven't seen one.

—There was one on the racecourse, following the horses round.

—A brewery lorry counts, Harry said.

—And jockeys? Margaret said.

—Jockeys, but not proper people, Harry said.

—How much do they count for? Margaret asked. But she did not wait to hear.

Now the cars began to move again, nosing out into the main road and accelerating up the hill. The shadow of the house fell across the lawn and the road. A flag above the grandstand caught the last of the sun and stretched and flapped and the traffic policeman waved his white arms. Mr Toms swung through his garden of jockey-bright flowers, watering his plants with a hose: through the blowing spray a rainbow arched. Mr and Mrs Lenihan came through the gate.

—Hallo, cried Mr Lenihan, breezy and boozy, up from the gate. Have you made a pile?

—Hallo, they said in unison, descending.

—We nearly made a killing, Mr Lenihan said. But the judge was a blind man.

—A blind man on a left-hand course, Mrs Lenihan said in the voice of one repeating a lesson.

Remembering that Mr Toms had been blind since his fall, Margaret looked to see if he had heard. She looked to where the spray was drifting back over the beds of flowers, but Mr Toms had gone. She followed her father into the house where his gaiety hammered in all the rooms. Under the gaiety she mused, nursing mournfully yet with delight a vision of the silk and velvet colours falling spread out through the silent circle, falling to the silent grass. It might have been a vision of death, multi-coloured and fantastic and benign, from which—smothering her in wonder—silence had taken all but the charm. But she did not know. On the short grass the colours had lain so still.

Mr Lenihan was quiet. He pushed himself up from his chair and crossed the darkened room to where she sat. In a pale recollection of his former gaiety he smiled.

—Ah well, he said, the judge is a blind man, and that's that. A blind man, only, he joked to her wondering face.

The Bull

HELEN SHAW

Miss Valentine, staggering under the weight of a great hamper basket, burst out of the hall of the house onto the verandah, defiantly attempting to look less than her years in flamboyant scarlet, but in blissful ignorance of the black petticoat that was dipping down below her gaudy hemline.

'There you are, father dear,' she warbled, brushing Mr Valentine's ear with her grey curls as she kissed him.

'I've told you before to be careful of my ear, Lulu, *careful!*' the old man snapped back. Cantankerous as usual, he sat in the sun in his pyjamas and plum coloured velvet coat near the red and blue glass that closed in one end of the verandah. And where was his daughter going with 'her cabin trunk' he inquired sarcastically, then, when she said it held currants she had picked for a neighbour, he scoffed and groped through his pockets for the brush to groom his venerable dog. 'Why don't your friends cultivate their own garden, my girl?' he asked as he explored his dog's black and tan coat for fleas. 'Sit up, Skipper, and listen to the human race following-my-leader calling baa, baa, baa, just listen to us, sir,' Mr Valentine mimicked, menacingly smacking up clouds of dust from the tartan rug tucked round his knees. 'I'll remind you, Lulu, you're standing *in my sun,* girl, in my *s-u-n*,' he bellowed suddenly.

'Now, father, I'll only be gone a minute, father, really father,' Miss Valentine said gaily, and hovered over him, kissed the white plume on his bald head, then hurtled across the tennis court in youth's gaudy colours that so accentuated her age.

The Valentines' dog stretched itself, rose, and walked round in a circle, an unforgettable smell wafting up from its body, then it yawned and lay down, servile nose on its master's boot.

Through his binoculars Joseph Valentine watched his daughter retreating into the shrubbery. 'There goes a supporter of lost causes, sir,' he said, talking down to the dog and thinking of the dining room walls that were plastered with Lulu's paintings of waterfalls and pungas. 'Pungas! Scatter my ashes over the honest to God tussocks, Skipper, and preserve me from the sly, dripping green bush,' he shivered, 'though I suppose she enjoys herself, sir,' the old man continued, his voice becoming more charitable as the sun warmed his hands.

He sat very still staring at bees crawling in and out of the geraniums that lapped the edge of the verandah. He could see them cleaning their thin, active legs. Legs! He hadn't the strength for skylarking left in *his* legs. 'And the whole place to ourselves, sir,' Mr Valentine grunted, but the dog, bothered by flies, scratched its rump half-heartedly and snored off to sleep again, and soon the old man followed suit, falling rapidly into a light nap of troublesome dreams.

Back again in the Supreme Court he found himself defending his great-grandfather, Ebenezer Valentine, for an unknown and mysterious crime, with magnificent eloquence until old Judge Y. intimated it was futile proving a dead man's innocence, but would Joseph rid the Court of the bees that were swarming in a corner of the gallery, whereupon Joseph gallantly removed his wig and pitched it overhand into the heart of the swarm which caused one bee to sail down straight into Joseph's eye and sting him so that he couldn't move, speak or breathe. Softly, softly he crumpled up and fell down at Judge Y.'s feet, paralysed.

'What the devil's the meaning of it, sir?' Mr Valentine snapped, as he woke with pins and needles to find the dog up on his knees. 'Down, sir,' he commanded, and it was then old Joseph saw the bull—an enormous, cinnamon brown, dirty cream, hulking brute, all ugly head and shoulders, glaring at him out of the geraniums with mean, unpredictably mean eyes —and less than a couple of yards between himself and the danger.

'Almighty God,' the old man swore, as he laid his stiff, mittened fingers on the dog's snout. 'It's going to be a case of mind over matter, over matter, do you see, Skipper, over matter,' he babbled, still keeping his eyes on the bull and feeling excitedly around for his binoculars, at the same time trying to steady his feet in preparation for the move he had got into his head was essential. Slowly the old barrister rose up out of his bursting leather chair that for years had been disgorging horsehair.

'Forgive us our sins and trespasses, and trespasses,' he repeated until he had his spindly legs under control, then up he swung the binoculars and hurled them backwards through the coloured glass behind his head. The window broke and the bull bellowed. Its head went down, but then it lumbered round into a wanton retreat crashing over precious shrubs and tearing its way like a tornado through hedges.

Never in all his life had the old man felt so cold. His head seemed empty, his fingers were like ice; he slapped his dog's sides and pulled its ears for warmth and friendship, then set off along the verandah in his queer, high-stepping way to see the men who swarmed in from the street with ropes and pitch-forks settle their account with the recalcitrant bull, and presently was rewarded with a view of the captured beast being led away meek as a lamb.

Now was the Valentines' garden emptied of danger and filled with the aftermath of alarm as Lulu rushed towards old Joseph screaming, 'Dear father, coming father, speak to me father,' and stumbled up onto the verandah throwing freckled, sun-burned arms round his scraggy neck. 'Father, speak to me,' she panted. 'Father!'

He snapped his violet lips shut in her flaming face and pro-ceded inside, very shaky, but leaning on her until they reached the high-ceilinged, bottle-green bedroom where he undressed and climbed up into the double bed and stretched out under linen sheets and a crackling white counterpane.

'What are you looking at? Don't stare at me,' he roared. 'Brandy! And a hot bottle! And don't dream, girl,' he bellowed, as with a glaring blue, glittering eye he observed her scuttle from the room dropping numerous hairpins as she ran.

He slid his teeth into the mug of water on the cabinet and wound up his watch, then, beginning immediately to fume, he reached for his stick at the head of the bed and thumped hard on the floor with it for Lulu's services, but the moment she appeared he closed his eyes and foxed until she had supplied him with his brandy and hot bottle.

'And eighty-nine next June,' he boasted, when she had been and gone for the last time, and he sat up in bed and looked at himself in the mirror and stroked his moustache and swallowed his brandy, recalling how he had battled with the bull, when suddenly he heard the verandah window breaking again and the noise of glass splintering inside his head. 'The devil, what's that?' he cried, and poked into his ear, but in spite of his strong will and his patriarchal pride and arrogance, again the window broke; and broke and broke and broke inside his head, as if once was not enough to impress Joseph Valentine with the wonder of his aged body that still had breath left in it. Finally, like a warning voice that is carried out to sea by the roaring of waves, the tinkling of the glass grew fainter and fainter, became but a small echo wandering through colossal caves and then was lost, so that at last the old man was able to rest.

With the sheet drawn up to his chin, Joseph lay staring at a fly that buzzed inanely round and round in slow circles round and round above his snowy plumed head until at last the noise of his triumphant sleep filled the whole house with a mighty crescendo of thanksgiving.

Lolly-Legs

JANET FRAME

Lemmy Wheen lived mostly in two places, the railway station and the wharf, and nearly every day he could be seen going from one place to the other, sometimes walking slowly with his head down and his hands clasped behind his back; other times with his head out like a duck and his hands flapping, racing against the train while all the little boys on the street cried out, 'Go it Lemmy! Go it Lemmy!' Yet no matter how hard Lemmy went it the train always won. But why should he race the train? Why should he do anything? What did he think about? No one really knew for Lemmy could not speak. He made strange noises that were not speech, only a kind of singing cry. He was not all there, folks said, his mouth was made funny, he could hear all right, and at times he knew what you said to him, but he wasn't all there, and that was why he lived on a pension already, a boy of twenty-five who would never come out as anything, only hang around the railway station watching the train and picking up the empty bottles; or on the wharf lording it like an admiral whenever the dirty orange and black wheat boats were docked in.

Lemmy's third place to live was his Aunt Cora's house, two-storeyed, with venetian blinds. Lemmy's bed was there and his toy ships and trains in his bedroom. And every morning his plain, wholesome breakfast, at midday his lunch, and evening his dinner. And there was Aunt Cora, fading and restless, her hair covered with a bright flowery scarf to hide the curling pins. 'For people will look over the gate, Lemmy, and see me and think I'm an old hag who curls her hair. And I'm not, am I?'

Lemmy wouldn't answer, of course. Sometimes he would

smile as if he understood, a big wide grin that his deformed mouth changed to a sneer one moment later. His mouth would not keep still, but twitched in a continual torment of near-speech.

And Aunt Cora would continue her favourite topic of Aunt Cora. 'Let the people look over the gate. I've a home of my own, two-storeyed. I've a radio of my own, carpets, all paid for. I've a wicker rocking chair, too, and although wicker rocking chairs are out of date they're nice to rock in. And I've given shelter to a homeless child. Lemmy, people keep talking about your going on the station and the wharf all the time, be a good boy and stay with your toy trains and boats at home.'

And Lemmy would listen with his fingers pressed against his lips and his eyes staring in a vacant way. Then he would laugh and give a wailing kind of cry like the cry a swamphen makes out of the mist in the early morning; and then he would be off down to the station for the train.

'The train will depart in two minutes' time. All seated, please!' It is no use to grab a black shining monster and hold on to it. The people kiss and wave and climb in and the train is gone. Then begins Lemmy's real work. A moment ago the train had blocked sight of the sea. Now in the foreground there is a glittering blue and green strip of sea like light on a screen. And the seagulls have come to play at being people. They swoop noisy and querulous to the platform where the broken and sodden bits of fruit cake lie half sunken in muddy yellow saucer lakes of tea. They pick eagerly at odd floating peninsulas of crust attached to a mainland of ham or egg sandwich. Lemmy's as busy as the gulls. He grabs the necks of lemonade and ginger ale bottles and rushes to the refreshment room for threepence a bottle. He gathers the cups for the waitress, who gives him in return a plate of left-over sandwiches. Lemmy's as busy as a clock and then suddenly everything's over and there's nothing to be on the station for and the seagulls fly back to the beach. The keeper of the sandwiches seems tired and irritable. She slops up wet tea from one of the clean tablecloths and tells Lemmy Wheen to clear off in the name of heaven and stop being a nuisance. She signals with her hands. Lemmy understands but cannot speak his understanding. He sets out for the wharf. There is no train to race, so he wanders along blinking at the sun and the cars and the few people. He's like a ship that has called at a port to load cargo and finding the wrong cargo or the port closed must journey elsewhere, perhaps miles and miles, to a new place, the wharf and the sea. But all things are journeys, some that never finish, like Lemmy's beginning to speak and saying no words.

It was the not speaking that worried Aunt Cora so much that she resolved one day to do something about it. The not speaking and the wandering around the station and the wharf, why, anything could happen to the boy. After all, she thought, he'll just go on and on, and I'll just go on and on and never have a real life of my own. It's time I had a life of my own. With her home and radio and carpets Aunt Cora had gained practice in ease of possession. Now she had an unshakable though perhaps unwarrantable faith in an easy life of her own, nothing to pay, either, no weekly instalments and forms to sign. Each night now Aunt Cora would look across the table at Lemmy and wonder. Lemmy was so much like his father, Captain Lemmy, who had been drowned at sea. His father was always journeying somewhere back and forth; no wonder the poor lad was fond of trains and boats. But he wasn't right in the head, the poor lad. There's a place for those folk, thought Aunt Cora. They're nice places. He'll learn to be useful and weave and do woodwork. Some of them make baskets. And I certainly must have a life of my own.

So Aunt Cora made arrangements for everything, and one day when Lemmy came from the railway station to home, a port of call before going on to the wharf, he found a tasty lunch on the table. There was a big bun like a wheel snowed under with coconut right in the middle of the table between him and Aunt Cora. With the coconut bun and the teapot and speech separating them Aunt Cora told Lemmy about the new place where he would be going. Why had she worried? Lemmy grinned and made his peculiar bird-like cry, then he reached for a segment of the monstrous circular bun and stuffed it in his mouth. And then calm as noon he ambled to the bedroom while Aunt Cora showed him the new suitcase she had bought for him. She lifted the lid from the deep red emptiness. Sometimes when Lemmy was younger she used to cook something nice and show it to him cooking. She would lift the lid of the saucepan. Lemmy would lick his lips and peep in on something, there was always something there. But the suitcase held nothing and smelt of nothing and there was Aunt Cora standing with her hand on the lid and smoothing proudly and possessively over the soft leather that held nothing to be tasted or taken hold of or looked at. Lemmy turned and picked up the black beret one of the wharfies had given him and Aunt Cora knew he was going to the wharf. How could she stop him? He could look after himself in the traffic or he seemed to be able to, but it was all a terrible tie. But tomorrow by the third bus, no, the eleven-thirty would be better. . . .

Aunt Cora went to the wardrobe and prepared to pack Lemmy's clothes. Everything was ready, really. Let the poor boy have a last look around the wharf.

When Lemmy arrived at the wharf he always hurried first to the edge to look at the sea and the waves that elbowed each other in their continual journeying. The sea departed always, not just in two or three minutes' time. It came in always beating against the kauri piles and then later, quiet and remorseful, licking the deep cracks that gaped like wounds in the side of the aged kauri logs. And then it would break on the rocks at the other side of the wharf, and although the rocks stood up jagged and fierce the salt water did not tear or bleed but stayed whole and shining.

Who knew what Lemmy Wheen thought or dreamed as he watched the sea? He was standing there staring this afternoon when the wharfies passed. There was the captain of the boat, too, in gold braid. 'Hy-ya, Lemmy,' the wharfies cried, 'Hy-ya, Lemmy.'

Lemmy's bird cry broke from him and the captain turned to look. He called one of the wharfies over and questioned him. They stood beside Lemmy and Lemmy listened. Who knows what he heard or understood?

'By jove, that's Lemmy Wheen's son. I sailed with Lemmy Wheen. You couldn't beat Captain Wheen. We used to call him Lolly-Legs. I heard somewhere about his son.'

The wharfie turned to get on with his work but the captain continued talking. The wharfie lit a cigarette. After all, on a day like this, and there's always overtime.

'Yes, we called him Lolly-Legs.' The captain's voice rolled from side to side as if it were on board ship and trying to keep balance. 'He broke his leg once and while it was still in plaster he used to get around with a piece of red stuff tied around it. He looked like one of the peppermint walking sticks you buy.'

He fished in his pocket and held up a peppermint stick. 'I always have one somewhere. Sticky, but it's a quirk o' mine to

remember Lemmy. If ever a man was a born sailor it was
Captain Wheen. Lolly-Legs. But I'd better be off. Don't you
believe it, but the cook gets better pay than I do.'

The captain strolled away and the wharfie stubbed out his
cigarette and made for the cranes and tarpaulin-covered trucks.
Lemmy still looked at the sea. The sky was blue and the water
shimmered. There would be dogfish down in the water, little
apologies for sharks, and then later at teatime the red cod
when the fishing boats snuffed and chugged home around the
breakwater. And then the one winking eye of the harbour light
would shine.

Lemmy didn't stay to help around that day. He picked up a
handful of wheat and stuffed it in his pocket, then dawdled along
past the boat, across the railway line. He was going home. There
was a wooden ship in his bedroom. He would sail in it. He
would sail in it on every sea in the world.

He passed the shop at the corner and looked in the window.
There was a fly sitting on a piece of cardboard and beside the
cardboard was a peppermint stick red and white, the sort that
the Captain had held up to show the wharfie. Lemmy went
into the shop and pointed to the stick in the showcase.

The shopgirl put down her knitting and came over. She
stared at Lemmy.

'Well?'

Lemmy still pointed to the peppermint stick. Then he put
on the counter the threepence he had been given for a bottle.
He didn't ever go shopping, but he knew the little silver money
that could be put down on the counter in exchange for things.
The shopgirl shook her head. 'It's not enough. They've gone up,'
she said abruptly. 'Anything else you fancy?'

Lemmy let out his strange cry, his mouth twitched and he left
the shop and walked slowly up the street. The wheat kept
dropping from his pocket until there was a thin gold trail
behind him, like the trail of crumbs the story character left so
as to find the way back. But in the story the birds flew down
and ate the crumbs and there was no way back.

One World

PHILLIP WILSON

Along the river bed, in the paddock that ran down from the red clay bank to the edge of the water itself, the grass was high and thick and brown in its summer deadness, so tall that it came to his waist almost, the dry stalks sticking into his bare legs and the pollen dust, as he walked, rising into his nose in the warm still afternoon air. The track was so overgrown that he was going mainly by instinct, although he wasn't sure what place he was heading for or what his purpose was until suddenly, rising apparition-like above a clump of yellow ragwort flowers, he saw the house. He knew only Maoris could live in it. The river bed was their land, even if they didn't farm it, except for a plot of sweet corn which he had passed a moment ago, already stripped and weed infested. A long-maned pony was tied underneath a walnut tree by the sagging fence.

He was still squatting silently when he heard someone approaching. There was no sound of footsteps, nothing but the thin musical hissing of a man whistling to himself between his teeth, when abruptly and so close that he stood up in astonishment, came the swish of grass being pushed aside, and a yard away from him he saw Jimmy Hotene.

'Hullo, Ken,' the man said.

'Is this where you live?'

'That's right. I live here with my mother. Just the two of us and old Bingo. He's probably asleep now or he would have started barking.'

'I didn't know the river was your property.'

'It isn't mine,' Jimmy said. 'It really belongs to the tribe. But we live here. What you doing so far from home?'

'Exploring.'

Jimmy pushed out with the tip of his tongue the single false tooth that was fixed where he had been kicked in the mouth at a football match. He put a hand up and scratched his hair behind one ear with his little finger, then started whistling again.

'Why don't you come over?' he said.

The boy followed him through the grass towards the house. He went inside. It was only one room, with two beds against the walls and a table of unpainted wood and two broken kitchen chairs. By the cold fireplace, in an armchair so decrepit it must have been picked up on some rubbish heap, an old Maori woman was sitting with her eyes closed. A brown dog lay curled at her feet. When Jimmy came in the woman opened her eyes and the dog lifted its head and gave a hoarse, rheumy bark.

'Who you got?' the woman said.

'This here is Ken Roberts,' Jimmy said. 'Ropata's boy. He's been out exploring.'

'What?' the old woman said. She looked at him with her slate-coloured eyes. 'He here?'

'He's run away from home,' Jimmy said.

'No I haven't.'

'He's come to see us,' Jimmy said.

The woman closed her eyes.

'Not often that anyone comes out here,' Jimmy said. He sat down on one of the broken-backed chairs and rested his elbows on the table. 'No school today, hey? Saturday.'

'You see Mary?' the old woman asked.

'She's coming over later. She's bringing you some tea and some beer, maybe.'

It was warm in the room. The boy stood in the middle of the floor, by the table.

'Your father know you're here?' Jimmy asked.

'No,' the boy said. He looked at the old woman, who had her eyes closed as if she lived in a perpetual state of drowsiness. The dog yawned and stood up, shaking itself with incredible antique slowness.

'Hullo, Bingo,' Jimmy said. The dog tottered towards him. 'He's fifteen,' Jimmy said to the boy. 'Ever see a dog that old before? Older than you are.'

'No,' the boy said.

'Well, this is where I live,' Jimmy said. He looked around the room. 'It's not much of a place, but I was born here.'

The boy stood by the table, resting one hand on it. He said nothing.

'Play football for the school yet, Ken?' Jimmy asked.

'First fifteen,' he said. He lifted his head and looked into Jimmy's eyes.

'In the scrum?'

'No. On the wing.'

'That's the place,' Jimmy said. 'That's where I play.'

'Yes'.

He heard a woman singing outside, and a Maori girl came in. She was small and light-skinned, walked with a springing cat-like swing, and carried a basket in her hand, a flax kit. She took out a large newspaper bundle and two bottles of beer which she placed on the table. She looked at the boy but didn't greet him. He smelt the fish and chips.

'This for you, old lady,' the girl said.

The woman's slaty eyes slid in her direction.

'You be old one day too,' she said. She hadn't raised her voice, but the girl wriggled and looked at Jimmy.

'I'm hungry, by crikey,' Jimmy said.

The girl unwrapped the fish and chips. She took off the outer layer of newspaper and put some of the steaming pieces of fish and a handful of chips in it and carried them over to the old woman.

'Eat,' she said.

Mrs Hotene grabbed a piece of fish and began to chew it, spitting bones on to the mat. Jimmy placed the cap of one of the beer bottles against the edge of the table top and banged down on it with his fist. The cap flew off. The girl put three cups on the table and Jimmy filled them with beer. He pushed the fish and chips on the newspaper towards the boy.

'Hungry?' he said. 'You can have some.'

The boy took a chip but didn't put it in his mouth.

'I'd better be going home,' he said. Then he put the hot salty chip in his mouth and chewed.

'Yes. Be dark soon,' Jimmy said. 'You hurry home.'

The boy looked at the three Maoris. 'Goodbye,' he said.

'Good fun, exploring, eh?' Jimmy said.

'Yes.'

'Remember. Go for that corner flag.'

He went out and started to run along the almost imper-ceptible path through the grass. After a while he slowed to a walk. His heart was thumping and his knees were beginning to smart where the dry grass stalks had pricked them. It was still light when he got home. He went into the bathroom and washed his hands and sat down at the kitchen table. His father looked up through his spectacles over the newspaper he was reading.

'Where have you been this afternoon?' his father asked.

'Exploring.'

'By yourself?'

'Yes,' the boy said. 'I've been to Jimmy Hotene's place.'

'Is that so?' His father looked at him for a moment. 'Was he home?'

'Yes.'

'What happened?'

'We had fish and chips. His mother was there, and another girl.'

'That would be Mary,' his father said. He folded up the paper. 'You don't want to go there too often, though.'

'All right.'

'Did you talk about football?'

'Yes.'

'Jimmy's the best wing three-quarter this district has ever had,' his father said. 'Whatever he tells you will be good advice.'

The boy began to butter his bread. 'Yes,' he said.

It was winter then and he went to see Jimmy play at Rugby Park, standing in the rain eating a hot meat pie beside his impeccably overcoated father, stern and immobile apart from the darting eyes in his bleak puritan face. He watched Jimmy sprint down the sideline with his chin out, his mouth open and his teeth set, and the air whistling through the gap where that solitary denture had been removed before the game began. The crowd cheered him on.

'He's a match winner, that boy,' his father said. 'We wouldn't be so good without Jimmy to score the tries.'

That night from his bedroom he heard his father talking. It was something about a girl, the daughter of a farmer who lived down the Longfern Road. Jimmy had been taking her to dances, and now there were rumours, whispers around the town. It was difficult to make out what was being said from the darkness of the bedroom, then his father's voice came clearly through.

'She likes him because of his football blazer.'

Next time at the Park Jimmy wasn't playing. His father said nothing about it, but everyone cheered the new wing three-quarter running towards the corner flag. Later he stood on the edge of the main street, waiting for his father who had gone into the hotel, when he saw Jimmy coming towards him. But he had changed. The boy could see it, the gloom and discontent in Jimmy's face as he half rolled, half limped along the footpath.

'How are you today?' he said.

'I'm like a boot, full,' Jimmy said. He breathed beer into the boy's face, pushing out with his tongue tip the single denture. He hiccupped. 'Nothing to do on a Saturday afternoon in town these days.'

'How's your mother?'

'I think she will die soon,' Jimmy said. 'She very tired.'

'What are you doing now?'

'I haven't had a job since Friday.'

He knew that Jimmy's mother still lived down on the river bed, that she was almost blind now but had somehow endured in defiance of the death which by rights should have been hers, brown and shrunken, occasionally appearing in the streets with a whalebone walking stick and a black silk handkerchief over her head, moving with slow steps in her cracked black shoes, in an ankle-long gown of black satinette. The blue moko tattoo on her chin was the visible symbol of her age and her authority among the Maoris who lived at the pa, as she talked quietly in a lamenting voice to those who stopped to pass the time of day with her, shaking hands gravely with all, rubbing noses with the older ones, a matriarch and proud of her son's fame as a rugby player. He could understand that she would be feeling tired now.

'I'm sorry Bingo died.'

'Me too,' Jimmy said. 'He the best dog I had.'

The boy looked across the street but his father hadn't appeared yet from the swinging brass-handled door marked Private Bar in black letters across its opaque glass panel. Jimmy was looking at the ground. He was rocking slightly back and forth.

'How many points did you score last season?' the boy asked.

'Sixty-nine,' Jimmy said. He stopped rocking. 'Sixty-nine last season. And twenty-seven this.'

'You'll score more.'

'No,' Jimmy said. 'Too much beer. Not in the team now.'

He began to walk away, going in the direction of the railway lines where he would cross the fields that led to the river, big, shambling and desolate-seeming like some blinded mahogany Samson.

'How's Mary?' the boy called to him.

'She's fine.'

Jimmy smiled. The smile seemed to spread until the whole lower half of his face was shining with white teeth. He waved and went on, no longer swaying, and the boy turned and watched the swinging hotel door once again.

He left school and went away to Auckland to the university. One summer holiday when he came back he met Mary in the street. He hardly recognised the girl who had brought fish and chips that afternoon to the shanty and whom Jimmy had married, so he had heard. She was smartly dressed, with high heels and silk stockings, and she had with her on the pavement two children, both boys. Though he had never spoken to her he now stopped and asked for news of Jimmy.

'He doing all right,' Mary said.

'Is he still playing football?'

'No. He work in the mill down at the forest. He not come home much.'

'How's Mrs Hotene?'

'She dead.'

Mary walked away down the street, followed by the two shiny-haired ragged boys with eyes as large and brown as chocolates.

A week later his father told him that Jimmy was in gaol. The police had picked him up at Rotorua.

'What's he done?'

'Any number of things,' his father said. 'As far as I can gather, what they have got him for is converting a car. He's turned into a wild no-good sort of fellow. Deserted his wife and children, never comes to the old home town any more.'

'It's a pity he gave up playing football.'

'He had to, after he started drinking. There was some trouble about a girl named Jess Matthews, you may have heard of her. I believe she was in the family way. Of course her parents are proud people, and even if she had been so wayward as to consort with a Maori, they wouldn't let her marry him. So Jimmy began to get drunk every night.'

'Is that what spoilt his game?'

'I believe that was the cause of it.'

'What happened to Miss Matthews?'

'She went to stay with relatives in another part of the country. She hasn't come back yet,' his father said.

He saw Jimmy once after that, when he had graduated from

the university and had come home to join the family law firm. He was watching a game at the Park and noticed standing nearby in a battered felt hat and torn overcoat a gigantic fat Maori who, despite his bloodshot eyes and down-at-heel appearance, seemed to be taking a keen interest in the game. It wasn't until the man pushed out the single denture with his tongue tip that he recognised him.

'Hullo, Jimmy,' he said.

The bloodshot eyes gleamed with an emotion that was more like fear than friendship. But the old steady voice was the same.

'Hullo, Ken. Come to see the big game, eh?'

'Do you think we will win?'

'We can always win,' Jimmy said.

But that was all. There was no smile this time. The sun came out briefly from behind the cloud and shone in their faces. Jimmy tilted his hat forward.

'Damn sun hurts my eyes,' he said.

'Ever get a game these days?'

'Not me. I coach the kids. Soon they play for us too, eh?'

When he got home he said to his father, 'I saw Jimmy Hotene on the bank this afternoon.'

'You did? How was he looking?'

'Pretty seedy. But he loved the game.'

'Good old Jimmy,' his father said. 'He's working as a day labourer now, digging ditches, shovelling gravel. But you can't keep him away from a football game. I bet he hasn't missed one this season.'

'Is he still living with Mary?'

'Still in the same place down on the river bank. You remember it, don't you?'

'Yes.'

'Those boys of his are a couple of smart young scamps. We might have some good material there.'

'Not as good as Jimmy though.'

'You may be right,' his father said. 'Big Jimmy certainly was a flier.'

'He was the best wing three-quarter this town has ever known.'

'I agree with you.' Then his father made a curious gesture of disdain and despair. 'He might have done great things if he hadn't got himself mixed up with that Matthews girl.'

Aunty Wai's Wedding

NOEL HILLIARD

For three weeks before Aunty Wai's wedding the house was in
a turmoil. Women were coming and going all the time, holding
long conferences in the front room about kinds of material and
matching colours, who were to be bridesmaids, who would be in
charge of collecting different things for the hui. Bubby was
forever making cups of tea, fetching catalogues with samples of
cloth, trying to find the tissue-paper patterns that Mum had
hidden away years before. Meals were never on time. Dad
sneaked in and out as if he were a boarder in his own home; he
and Paikea took to spending most of their evenings with the
storm-lantern down in the garage, tinkering with the car.

Bubby stood around holding pins, fetching cotton while Mum
ran up the bridesmaids' dresses on her machine. She had ordered
special material from town for her matron-of-honour's dress, and
it turned out to be so nice that she was afraid of spoiling it and
asked Auntie Emma, who had once worked as a machinist in
town, to cut and sew it for her. The night she phoned the measurements through, Bubby stood close enough to hear the voice
at the other end.

'Chest, forty-seven. . . .'

'*Ho*-ly *heck!*'

'Waist, forty-two and a half. . . .'

'*Cri*-key *dicks!*'

'Hold on . . . hips, fifty-three. . . .'

'*Boy* oh *boy! What?*'

'Well, I want it tight, you know.'

'You don't say!'

'And leave plenty room in the sleeves.'

'Are you sure you didn't put the tape around the water-tank
by mistake?'

For Wai's wedding present Mum bought a pressure-cooker. 'What you want to get that thing for?' Dad scoffed. 'What's wrong with the hangi? The Maori invented the pressure-cooker!' Mum liked it so much she kept it for the house and bought Wai a set of pots instead.

One night twelve of the family were gathered to fold four hundred dainty paper serviettes. They sat at the table and on the floor while Mum demonstrated: 'First you fold it a bit one way, then you turn it around and do it a bit the other way, about the same, and so on you go that way till at last you spread it like a fan, wet your fingers and twist the middle part together, then stand it up, with the spoon at the bottom to hold it.' The men with their thick farmers' hands found it hard to get used to; they worked in solemn silence while the women stole glances at them, chuckling. Paikea was all fingers and thumbs. At last he threw a torn serviette on the floor and stamped on it.

'Serviettes! What a stupid Pakeha idea! Serviettes—for Maoris! They'll eat with their fingers anyway!'

Later, the children were sent out while the grown-ups discussed whether Wai should wear white or not. Mum and the other relations wanted white, but some of the older women, and the vicar's warden, were insisting on a colour. 'What's it got to do with all them what Aunty Wai wears?' Bubby asked. 'It's something you'll find out by and by,' Mum said. So they sat on the veranda playing Last-card while the voices hummed on in the sitting-room for nearly an hour. Towards the end they could hear Dad, and he sounded as if he had his temper up: 'She can get married in her pyjamas if she wants to!' When Bubby was called in to take around the cakes for supper, she could tell from Mum's smile that white had won.

The wedding day was clear and bright; from the homestead Bubby could see past the school and the church all the way to Franklin's farm down on the coast hills. You could see that far only on the very clearest days.

After breakfast they set off in the car: past the turn-off, down the swamp road, past the lake and out on to the isthmus. The road was rough with potholes and ditches of sand scoured by wind off the sea; the old car bucked and rattled and with its muffler off puttered like a speedboat.

They stopped at the top of a hill. Dad looked at the tyre, tested it with spit on his finger. 'Only a leaky valve. A pumping's all it needs for today.' While Paikea pumped, Bubby crossed the road and sat on the lip of a cutting. Beyond the dunes of glistening white sand the sea was an intense blue; islands floated like purple cushions, and the cape lay like a grey cloud. She wished she could go over for a swim. Cars coming past stirred the dust; every car tooted as it passed, and the children heaped at the back waved through the window.

At the foot of the steep hills dividing the peninsula Dad took a right turn to the beach. There was no road here; you had to drive along the wet sand for a little way and turn up a cow-path into the valley through the hills; that was why the wedding had to be put off until the morning tide was right.

'I'm glad we found that flattie before,' Dad said. 'Just think if I stopped here to fix it, with all those people wanting to get past.'

Even at dead low water the turn into the valley was only a few feet from the surf. The car jigged over the rough ground, skidding in the wet clay and slewing sideways. They drove through tussock and scrub up a winding dirt road to the church on the hill.

'We made it!' Paikea sighed.

Dad looked at him angrily. 'Who said we wouldn't?' He patted the hot radiator. 'Course we made it!'

Trucks were lined up with tiny tots squatting on the back, looking around and saying nothing. The men sat along the low stone wall, watching the cars arrive; the women nursed babies, holding hats in the breeze. Big girls in bright dresses stood around barefooted and giggling. Some mares tethered to the fence were suckling foals, and dogs lay asleep in the shade of the scrub. Cars coming up the valley raised a tall cloud of dust. Bubby could follow their progress around curves and through cuttings without seeing them; and as they lurched up the hill, up the road cut deep by the run-off of summer rain, the people leaned together along the wall and said, 'Here's Henry . . . Sally . . . Harriet . . . Waiata . . . who's that next to Waiata in the back?'

It was a quarter past eleven and still no sign of the bridal couple. The Rev. Komaru pulled his vestments about him and said, 'I think those fellows must be going to have their feed first. Anybody else here want to get married?'

A taxi turned up the hill.

'Here he is—the man himself!'

It stopped at the gate in a cloud of dust. All the children came rushing to see. The groomsman got out first, sweating in his shiny suit; then the best man, fingering his pink tie. As the

bridegroom stepped out, everyone called, 'Good old George!' He
stood stooped and apologetic, hair gleaming with oil, shoving
his hands into his pockets and pulling them out again.

Komaru cleared his throat. 'Well, we can marry *you*, now that
you're here, even if we can't marry *her!*'

The children were chasing each other among the parked cars,
kicking up dust; the dogs stirred themselves and joined in,
yelping. On the back of a truck, guarding a kit of soft-drinks
between her knees, a kuia with a scarf over her head sat smoking.
The big girls walked in groups from baby to baby, smiling,
chin-chucking, ear-tickling, finger-poking at protruding bare
bellies while the mothers stood watching with complacent and
self-satisfied half-smiles.

A taxi decorated with white ribbon joggled up the hill. 'Here's
Wai now!' A vestryman went in to ring the bell—a thin cracked
sound only a little louder than the squeak of the rusty axle.
Women rushed to fetch cameras. Wai, white with nervousness,
stepped from the car.

'We better go in now,' Dad said. 'Bubby, you go behind the
bushes first.'

'I been!'

The church was decorated with vases of bright flowers. Light
from the stained-glass altar window coloured the faces of the
people in the front pews. There was loud, restless scuffing; men
stood at the back around the font, sharing prayerbooks. Komaru
took his place behind the altar-rails and motioned the bridegroom's party forward. While he deployed them in an inaudible
voice, the groom stood stunned and sheepish, trying to inhale
deeply in his tight waistcoat, looking around for an open window.

They began a hymn:

> *Tenei te atawhai*
> *A te Ariki nui;*
> *I tukua tona tinana*
> *Hei ora mo te ao.*

All heads turned, the singing became scattered as the bride
came in on her father's arm. Bubby hoped she would look her
way, so that she could give her a smile; but she walked slowly
past with her head down, looking at nobody. The two maids, in
blue, with posies of mixed pansies and violets, stared steadily
ahead as if walking along a balance-rail with a book on their
heads.

The singing picked up again and swelled in volume:

Me tuku tonu mai
Te Wairua o te pai
He ako nga ngakau nei,
E tango tika ai.

All knelt in prayer; there were howls from babies and loud hisses of 'Sssssshhh!' Komaru spoke rapidly in Maori; the congregation joined in the Lord's Prayer, a prolonged grumble with no distinction between words except for 'Ake-ake-ake-Amine.' Angry-looking women forced their way from the forward pews holding squalling children and excused themselves through the press of standing men.

In English, Komaru was leading the couple through their responses: '. . . for richer for poorer . . .' '. . . to love and to cherish. . . .' The best man pulled a handkerchief from his pocket and from its girth slipped the ring. Everyone stood on the prayer-rails to watch George put it on Wai's finger.

'. . . with all my wordly goods I thee endow. . . .'

Bubby noticed that Mum had started to cry; so had Mrs Harrison, and Aunty Charlotte, and Mrs Kingi. . . .

The couple knelt at the rails and the congregation eased itself awkwardly to its knees, with a banging of benches and squeak of pews. A screaming baby was taken out in a push-chair without tyres; its wheels clack-clacked loudly on the steps.

A prayer; a hymn; the blessing.

As the bridal couple followed Komaru down the aisle the women with cameras rushed to the door and stood aiming, hands shading the lens, heads twisting up and down. But the party turned instead to the vestry to sign the register; and the women blushed and giggled as the men, pouring through the doorway called, 'Here!—take one of me! I been married—ten years ago!'

There was a scatter among the cars, a rounding-up of children on to trucks, counting of heads, untethering of horses, whistling-up of dogs. A schoolboy in his first pair of grey slacks went among his mates saying, 'I got my long shorts on!'

The couple came from the vestry and posed for pictures. The groom shook hands, and women lined up to kiss the bride. 'Here!' old Toi called to those at the end, 'Kiss me—nobody waiting!' Bubby was surprised that the two looked no different now that they were married: George awkward and unsmiling, Wai limply shy.

Komaru, coming through the gate in a gust of wind, pushed his robes down with quick movements of his arms and shouted, 'Go 'way, wind—the people might see my petticoats!'

The couple headed for the beribboned taxi, sidestepping to avoid confetti, George feinting with his arm as if someone were trying to tickle him. Cameras clicked as they drove away. The old men, the wiseacres, the kaumatuas who had been through it all half a century ago, pulled their thumbs from their pants-tops and moved away.

'Next stop—the hui-house!'

Down the scrub road again, through dust: Dad had to stop two or three times to wait for a cloud to clear before taking a corner. The high hills, once cleared, had gone back to gorse and manuka. 'Lots of water-cress in the creek,' Paikea said. 'Why's it the cows don't get it like up home?'

'No cows, that's why,' Dad said. 'Used to be, one time. But with that rough drive along the sand-road the cream was very nearly butter when it got to the factory. They could never get better than second grades. So now they run sheep.'

The hui-house was on a mound above the sea in a clump of very old pohutukawas. The rusty roof-iron was twisted and the dry, grey boards had been prised loose by the hot sun and salt wind. Battens dangled loose along the slack fence and the gate lay rotting in the grass. On the hill behind were the fires with steaming billies of vegetables, a copper boiling, and heaps of fresh earth and manuka sticks where the hangis had been put down.

There were many more people here than at the church: all come for the feed and especially the toasts. Cars were parked at an angle to the sun and people were sitting on the grass in the shade of open doors or trying to make tents of blankets. Men stood at the backs of cars passing bottles from mouth to mouth. Groups merged into each other with hand-shaking, kissing, nose-pressing. 'Bubby! come and say hullo to your Aunty Sarah!' 'Paikea, here! kiss Ruby, she's your second cousin.' They were sick of all the kissing after a while—dozens and dozens of them, and some of the kids with Maori sores. 'Come on,' Paikea said. 'Let's go find fresh water get a drink.' They could find none; and when they returned the old kuia on the back of the truck had given out all the soft-drinks: the bottles lay dry and empty on the grass.

All on his own beside the gate stood Old Simon, tugging

at his white moustache, smiling benignly at the children with a
look to say, 'You!—why, I knew your grandparents.'

The hui-workers had been busy since six, carrying water, sorting out gear, cutting wood, slicing meat for the ovens. Now most
of them lay resting in the shade, hats over their faces, bottles
between their knees.

Komaru sat beside the door in the middle of a large group,
eager faces craned towards him. 'I was doing a wedding at
Anurangi,' he said. 'There was three couples getting married
all at once and I could only count four men at the altar. So I
said to one bridegroom, "Who's your best man?" "Me!" says
this fellow on the end. "Who's yours?" I ask the next one. "Me!"
says this same fellow again. He was the best man for the three
of them! I said, "This is a funny idea, I never heard of this
before. How you going to tell which ring?" "I got them all here"
—and he held up three fingers—"one, two, three! Starting from
the left!" '

The people roared.

'One of these fellows getting married was a widower, second
time up. When it came to placing the ring I notice he was
crying. "What's wrong with him?" I asked the bride. "I don't
know—better ask *him*," she said. "What's up?" I asked.
"Oh . . ." he says'—and Komaru sobbed—' "I'm thinking
about my poor dear first wife." "Too late to think about her
now!" I said. "She's gone, man. So come on!" '

Now the hangis had been opened and Wai's eldest brother
came from the hui-house. 'Bride and groom first! Now you,
Komaru! Kaumatuas!—step aside there, make room. All the
relations, shake it up! Aunties, uncles, cousins, all the rest of it!
Now anybody else who wants a feed!'

They trooped in, Bubby and Paikea to the children's table at
the side. They sat on long wooden benches at trestle tables, and
though all the windows were open the hall was like an oven.
Komaru's blessing on the food could hardly be heard above the
roar and banging. Wai and George sat at the top table, holding
hands, the big cake in front of them; they still looked as if somehow they had come to the wrong place and could hardly believe
it. They would live with Wai's people until George got a better
job than working in the quarry. They hoped to get a farm one
day.

Potatoes tasting of smoke, kumaras, a tablespoon of cabbage,
pork, a dob of stuffing, jelly, fruit salad. Cakes on the table, soft
drink, salt in saucers. Hands were shaken across tables, noses

pressed; in the huge hum of voices, 'Pass the tomato sauce' sounded like 'That's too much pork.' The children ate quickly and were wondering if they would get a second helping when Mum came bustling between the tables, a tea towel over her arm, calling 'If you've finished please leave, we want the second sitting in now.' Paikea hadn't finished; he was just starting his sweets when there was a shout at him because everyone else in the row wanted to get out. Twenty children stood packed against the wall and the only way out was past Paikea because the second sitting were crammed tight at the other end. He guzzled his food and turned his back on them, angry at the joggling and at leaving his second drink of orange untouched.

The grown-ups were changing over now; with the first sitting trying to get out and the second squeezing to get in and the waitresses pushing past with fresh food or trying to gather dirty plates, nobody was listening when Komaru came to the climax of his best story. In the back room they were tipping scraps into petrol drums; there was a frenzy of dish-washing.

Bubby stood panting outside the door. The hot still air of the valley was like a gentle breeze after the sticky heat of the hall.

The first sitting were lying on the grass discussing their feed.

'The hangis were in late. They've only opened one.'

'They weren't expecting half as many as this.'

'Terrible lot of outsiders—who'd think they'd travel so far?'

Paikea came down from the hall, pulling a face. '*Funny* feed, funny! I got one potato and a little-weeny bit of meat, all fat.'

There was a lot of drinking at the cars now. 'The toasts will be *later!*' Wai's big brother had shouted in the hall; and everyone was wondering how long *later* would be, because they'd waited so long in the sun for their dinner and there would be at least three sittings.

Old Simon, still leaning on his post, motioned them over. He took off his hat and wiped his bald head. 'I've been thinking, you can see everything from here.' He nodded towards a woman suckling her baby on a blanket under the pohutukawas: 'We get born.' He pointed to the hui-house: 'We get married.' He turned towards the cemetery on top of a ploughed hill across the valley; the graves had been cleared of bracken and rubbish but there were no flowers. 'And that's where we all finish up.' Bubby and Paikea felt uncomfortable; they looked from him to their feet, giggled and ran away.

'Let's look for kina.'

Down at the point the tide was changing. They found good-sized kinas under the rocks and left them heaped on Paikea's shirt while they had a swim naked. Paikea dived to see if he could find paua but instead he got a kina-spine under his fingernail. Bubby pulled it out, but the quick bled, and Paikea tried to suck out the stinging salt water.

Back at the hui-house the toasts had begun, they could tell by the roar and the ragged singing. They put the kinas in the car and went to see. The cake was being cut and people from different hapus were coming forward to sing for their piece. The place was jammed tight. Wai's big brother was finding it uphill work to keep a semblance of formality: there were side-conversations and a rush for glasses, those who'd had a drink were calling for more, and the cooks and helpers sitting around the kegs—plainly they'd not been allowed to get thirsty during the morning's preparations—were taking no notice. Attempts to get everyone singing were drowned in the roar.

Dad came out, swaying. He belched with dignity and made for the bushes.

They felt tired with the salt water stiff upon them after their swim, and decided to wait at the car. At the bottom of the hill they found the bridegroom, sitting on his own in the grass beside the road, his feet in the dry ditch, his head down; he looked just like someone waiting at the dentist's. There he was, just married, and on his own; nobody seemed to be in the least bit interested in him. And instead of going around among the people, greeting and shaking hands and laughing off their cheek, trying to enjoy himself, make the most of his day, there he was, sitting in the ditch, all by himself. He glanced up; his eyes were red and sullen. Bubby wondered if he'd had too much to eat.

The trucks and cars were starting to head off now. Mum and Dad carried down the pots, tea towels, jam dishes, cutlery, plates. The sun was well down in the sky. From the hui-house came a roar of singing: two or three songs all being sung at once.

'We might just catch the tide right, now,' Dad said. He headed down the valley. The car lurched over the dip into the sea; the wheels whirred and boiled in the surf.

'I picked it was going to be a hard-case turnout,' Dad said. 'That family of yours, they believe in looking after their own mob, never mind about anyone else. If you never had anything wet at the back of your car, it was just too bad for you.'

He turned up among the dunes, on to the sand-road. Bubby stuffed the tea towels among the plates and cups to stop the rattling.

'Yes, I saw all your relations staggering around on the hill, pickled. They won't go short, bet your life! When your old man came up to talk to me I thought he was going to invite me around the back to the family grog. But no! That'd be carrying hospitality too far, too far. . . .'

The children could see that Mum was building up for an explosion. Her pretty new dress was sopping wet from serving in the hall, washing up, running after people all afternoon.

But all she said was, 'You mean to say you only went over there to drink beer? You mean to sit here and tell me that?'

Dad leaned forward over the wheel, silent. Off the isthmus, past the lake, over the swamp road to the turn-off. After a quarter of an hour, Dad spoke. 'Course not. Nothing like that at all. Sorry I said anything.'

Instead of leaving the car at the shed he drove up the hill to the house to unload the gear. Inside, he threw his hat on the couch. 'Bubby . . . Paikea . . . you better do the cows tonight. I'm going to lie down for a while, I'm a wee bit tired. All that driving.'

When they came down from the shed two hours later they could hear his snores all the way from the calf-paddock gate.

The Mayor and Mrs McBride

DENNIS McELDOWNEY

The trees in the street were live things even in the dark, and they made a living thing of the street-light shining through their leaves. They mellowed it, broke it up, set it dancing; not at all like the cold glare it had been in the previous street. I sat and absorbed the effect for a moment after turning off the headlights on my car, because it was the trees I had come about. Then I ran up the path, knocked at the back door, and was confronted by Helen McBride, who was also alive.

She had dyed her hair black and for a moment I didn't recognise her. I stood politely and waited for the stranger to introduce herself. She stood and waited for me. Then her eyebrows shot up even higher than she had pencilled them originally and she laughed. There was no mistaking the laugh. Her laugh is a shattering thing. I sometimes fear for her kitchen window.

'I did it special for the Mayor,' she said, 'only it isn't me and I wish I hadn't.'

Her husband Bob sat beyond her on a yellow formica-backed chair at a yellow formica-topped table. He was reading the paper. 'She thought,' he remarked, 'she was going to look like Elizabeth Taylor, but she forgot she'd have to change her face as well.'

'Do you wonder I took to him with the poker last week?' Helen said, showing me into the kitchen and shutting the door. 'Mind you I was sorry afterwards it was the poker because it was a bit hard, but it had to be something and that was the only thing handy.'

'I called the police,' said Bob, still reading the paper, 'but they said they were too busy to come.'

Helen went back to the dishes, and to the cigarette she had

left smouldering on the window-sill, between the two china pot-bellied monks playing tennis.

'It's too late now,' she said, 'but I do think my natural colour suits the grace and refinement of my expression better. I'll go back to it tomorrow.'

'What is your natural colour?' I asked, running through all the shades from yellow, orange, red to chestnut. 'I've often wondered.'

Bob guffawed. 'Mousy!' he said. 'Mousy!'

'I was a platinum blonde, actual,' Helen said, 'when I was married.'

'Not when you married me you weren't,' Bob said.

Helen swung the dishcloth in his direction. It fetched instead her arrangement of spring bulbs on the primrose refrigerator. The arrangement was exuberant, like Helen herself. The vase, in addition, was low and narrow, and the whole thing top-heavy. It toppled slowly and gracefully from the fridge to the floor, where the vase flew into four unequal pieces and lay in a pool of water and daffodils. Helen flung the dishcloth on top of them, stood with her hands on her hips, breathed heavily through her nostrils, and gibbered.

Young Bobby, her eldest, popped through the kitchen door in his pyjamas, grinning from ear to ear, looked at the daffodils and listened expectantly. Helen eyed him sadly. 'Robert,' she said gently. 'My son. I have just knocked the flowers from the refrigerator and I was saying that-I-wished-I-had-not.'

'Yes, Mum,' said Bobby, still grinning.

'And if you aren't back in your flaming bed within half a flaming second you'll get a tanning you'll remember till you're ninety,' said his father. Bobby vanished.

'That,' said Helen, still sadly and quietly, 'is no way to speak to your son, Bob. Mother and father ought to be *consistent* in the upbringing of their children, and I have taken the gentle path.'

'Gentle!' said Bob. 'Since when?'

'Since tonight,' said Helen. 'I'm practising for meeting the Mayor.' She mopped up the water, tidied the four pieces of fluted china into the kitchen-tidy, shoved the daffodils into a preserving jar and went back to the sink. Bob lumbered to his feet and took up a dishtowel. I sat in his chair. It was time to get down to business.

'Got your petition ready?' I asked.

'Petition?' she asked. 'What for?'

'From the neighbours. To save the trees.' Speaking to her back topped by that nest of black hair I had to remind myself she was not a stranger to whom I should speak formally.

'Petition! If they signed a petition it would be to have them taken down. The leaves are a nuisance. Block the spouting.'

'So they do,' said Bob.

'Why the heck shouldn't they? What harm does it do? Easy enough to get them out. My theory is, they're scared.'

'Scared?' I said. 'What of?'

'Trees. Because trees are larger than they are. They want everything cut down to their own size. They don't even listen when I tell them they *need* trees. Because trees liberate chlorophyll into the air and—well you know what chlorophyll does. If it weren't for trees we just couldn't live with one another. Isn't that right, now?'

'It's a subject,' I said tactfully, 'I don't know much about.'

'Nor does my wife,' said Bob.

'Well, if you haven't got a petition,' I said, 'what are you going to do?'

'Do me scone,' she said. 'In,' she added, 'a ladylike manner. I must be refined. It'll be a strain, though. It's that little pointed beard and that voice. It'll be worse than having the minister to afternoon tea. Which nearly kills me.'

'I don't think you need worry about old Beasley,' I said. 'He isn't all that fearsome.' I'd offered to go with her to see the Mayor because I knew him slightly.

'So long as I don't say "bum",' she said. 'That's all I ask.'

The Mayor, who was a widower, lived by himself at the other end of the borough in a small bungalow fitted neatly under the branches of three large trees—an oak, an elm, and a walnut—which were now outlined, and lit up, and darkened with shadow, by the light from his front door. Helen took one look at this when we rose out of my car, and snorted: then she walked up the gravel path to the front door. She walked delicately, daintily. This worried me.

The Mayor received us and deposited us by the fire, with a courtly grace and a dead look in his eye. It was said the Mayor had at one time been alive, and that the beard and the shell of perfect manners were relics of that time. But it had been a long time ago; and his main qualification for the mayoralty was that it had been a long time ago. For his predecessor in the office had been in the habit of seizing councillors by the neck-tie or the coat-collar and dragging them round the council table, if they did not do what he wished. This had been felt by some to be a pity. Not so much of a pity that he was not re-elected every time he chose to stand; but when he finally retired sentiment favoured a change of manner. Hence the choice of Mr Beasley. Mr Beasley presided perfectly at council meetings. He spoke with gracious gestures, in words not his own, of the sewers. He began to perceive after his first year in office that it was now the councillors who, metaphorically, had *him* by the throat. This made him graver and more courtly than ever.

Helen sat in the armchair by the fireplace, her back as straight as a rod, her green shoes placed precisely together on the carpet, her hands folded in her lap. The Mayor sat in the opposite chair, eyeing her warily from his weary blue eyes. He was probably wondering, if he wondered anything at all, whether to believe me, who had told him Helen was a first-rate citizen and a devoted wife and mother; or his town clerk, who had told him she was a public nuisance. I sat between, facing the fire.

'You wanted, I believe,' said a voice from the Mayor, as if he had a gramophone inside him, 'to speak to me about the trees in your street.'

'Thank you, sir,' said Helen primly. 'It is gracious of you to allow me to express the united feeling of the street. Trees, in our opinion, have a beauty and a grace which is an inspiration to the young and a solace to the old.'

'They get in the way of the power lines,' said the gramophone rather weakly. 'The Power Board are constantly complaining.'

'They give,' said Helen, 'a breath of nature to a humdrum suburban street. We are always hearing people exclaim at the beauty of the trees in our street. They say there is no other street in the borough like it.'

'They are out of alignment for the footpath in the plan to reconstruct your street,' said the gramophone. 'We work, for reasons of economy, to a standard plan which makes no provision for trees already existing. They cannot be fitted into it.'

Helen's hands stirred a little in her lap at that and her lips tightened. She lost her thread.

'An inspiration to children,' she said, backtracking. 'They give them an idea of something larger and more serene than themselves in God's plan.'

'And encourage them to break their limbs,' said the Mayor, speaking off his own bat. 'And not only *their* limbs.'

'If any branches should come down, accidental,' she said with dignity, 'they are given to a dear old couple living nearby for firewood. And another advantage of trees is that they liberate chlorophyll into the air, and chlorophyll. . . ."

I coughed slightly at this point. I didn't think chlorophyll was going to help Helen's case. I didn't think she was making much of a case at all, but chlorophyll wouldn't help. They both looked at me, and Helen fortunately lost her thread again. Simultaneously the gramophone regained control over the Mayor.

'Wouldn't you welcome,' it said, 'instead of the untidy street you have now, neat concrete paths and kerbing and a velvety grass berm in between? It would lift the whole tone of the area. In a few years' time, when our finances become easier, we may plant smaller trees of a more suitable variety.'

'Bum!' said Helen.

'I beg your pardon?' said the Mayor.

Helen's hands were no longer folded in her lap. They were making stabs in his direction, alternately. 'You're talking nonsense,' she told him, informatively. 'You're saying things you don't believe a word of. If you did believe it, why do you live in the middle of a forest yourself?'

If the Mayor thought this was hitting below the belt he didn't say so. *'Touché!'* he said. Helen wasn't sure about the word but she was sure about the first sign of animation he had shown since we got there. She shattered the room with her laugh. Glass rattled all around us. She jumped up, stood over the Mayor, looking from my point of view like a column of green with a raven top.

'What the heck does it matter if trees are untidy?' she said. 'What does it matter? Nature's untidy isn't it?'

The Mayor rose out of his chair, almost sprang out of his chair. He seemed moved by her words, but not moved to talk any more about trees. Instead he took her by the arm and led her to the first of three glass cabinets which stood against three walls of the small living-room. These were full, as I knew well, of curios of a wandering youth. He opened the glass. He took out a dark brown bundle and unrolled it. It was the skin of a carpet snake. He wound it around himself to demonstrate how it crushed. He offered to let Helen wind it around herself. Helen screamed. He showed her rattles to tie around her ankles to keep devils away while dancing. He showed her grass skirts and castanets and model canoes and grotesque masks and a corpulent Buddha with a bowl in his lap. For a whole hour he led her around the relics of his youth, when he had been alive. She screamed and laughed and tried things on and listened to his stories and told me in stage asides what a wonderful man the Mayor was.

At the end of the hour the Mayor brought us china tea in fine china cups and said, as if it was a matter of little importance but ought to be cleared up, that her street would keep its trees if he had to drag the councillors round the table by their neckties to make them agree to it. At that moment he appeared to have no doubt that he could do it.

The Dark Angel

ALBERT WENDT

'We've got to make you look good for your mother,' the man said to his daughter, running a comb through her hair that hung down to her shoulders. 'Now, hold still, Emi.' The girl stood gazing into her father's eyes, sensing that something was wrong.

'Papa,' she asked, biting the end of her silk handkerchief, 'are we going to see mother soon?'

'Yes . . . now how's that?' he said, pushing her away and looking at her. The girl giggled, rushed forward, and embraced him. He bowed down and kissed her on the cheek. 'Now run along while I get dressed, then we'll go and see your Mamma,' he instructed, pushing her out the door.

'We're going to see Mamma, we're going to see Mamma!' she sang, as she skipped along the dark unpapered passageway toward her aunt's room. A dark little boy of about her age rushed out of the room and barred her way.

'Stop yelling,' he commanded her, standing arms akimbo. She poked out her tongue at him and went on singing and skipping. 'I'm going to tell my mother on you,' threatened the boy. The girl took no notice of him and kept up the noise. 'You're a tomboy . . . tomboy!' jeered the boy, changing strategy. 'You're wearing shorts. . . . Emi's a tomboy. . . .'

'Shut up,' interrupted the girl, advancing toward him. 'I'm not a tomboy.'

The boy continued to tease her, knowing that he had the offensive. The door behind him swung open, and a large woman, smoking a cigarillo, stepped into the passageway.

'Who was making all the row?' she asked.

'It was Edgar,' the girl replied immediately.

'I didn't. She did,' insisted the boy.

'He did, Aunt. He's lying.'

'I'm not,' argued the boy, knowing bitterly that he had lost the battle. 'She was making all the noise, Mummy.'

'You stop lying,' the woman said to the boy harshly. 'You hear me, you cut that lying. And you leave Emi alone. Go down and play with your brothers.' The boy wheeled angrily and stamped down the staircase. The girl giggled in victory.

'How do you like how Papa dressed me, Aunt?' she asked the woman, strutting before her like a model displaying a new creation.

'My, you look nice,' replied her aunt. 'Are you off to see your Mamma?' The girl nodded. The woman knelt down and embraced her tightly. The girl tried to squirm out of her aunt's embrace; she didn't like the way her aunt smelt.

'What's the matter, Auntie?' she asked, hoping her aunt would let her go.

'Nothing, Emi,' replied the woman, straightening up quickly. 'By the way, I've got something for your Mamma.' She turned and disappeared into her room.

The girl waited for her in the passageway, humming to herself.

'Here, this is for your mother,' her aunt said, handing her a small bunch of red roses.

'Thanks,' replied the child, suddenly liking her aunt for it was the first time her aunt had given her anything.

While the child buried her face in the dying roses, the woman stood above her like a soldier guarding something precious and fragile.

The door to the man's bedroom opened slowly, and he stepped out tall and pale, dressed in a neat charcoal grey suit that made him look like a preacher.

'Look!' the girl said to him, holding up the roses. 'These are for Mamma.' The man looked at the woman. She smiled at him.

'Thank you,' he said. The woman turned and retreated into her bedroom.

'What's the matter with Aunt?' the girl asked him.

'Nothing,' murmured her father, 'she's not feeling well today.' There was no strength in his voice. 'C'mon, we'll go and see your Mamma now.' He reached down, clasped her hand, and steered her up the passageway, out the door, and on to the street.

The sky was dark with clouds, leaves swirled round their feet, a cat skimmed across the road; a man, huddled in a tattered overcoat, brushed past them, as the wind licked at them and pushed them up the steep hill. The man walked, as soft as a shadow, not caring particularly about the things his daughter kept pointing out to him. The child clutched the roses tightly, afraid the wind might blow them away.

'This is a queer place, Papa,' she said. 'I wish we were back in Samoa.'

He pressed her hand, smiling down at her. 'So do I.'

It was the first time they had ever been outside Samoa.

They stood facing a six-storeyed building that was wrapped with wind, its red colour blurred by the rain. Then they crossed the road, mounted the steep path, and stood at the entrance of the hospital. The child looked back. The city shot out from beneath her feet and lost itself in mist.

'Is Mamma in there?' she asked her father, afraid of the size and silence of the hospital. He nodded.

The door of the lift clanged open, and a stream of people hurried from it and fled out the main entrance into the rising storm.

'What's that, Papa?' she asked, pointing at the lift.

'It is a moving box. It will take us up to see Mamma,' he said.

The palagi attendant called, 'Do you want to go up?'

'Yes,' the man replied in English.

'Let's go up with him,' his daughter whispered, pulling him towards the lift.

The attendant stepped aside and let them in. The door of the lift slid shut, and the man's arm closed protectively round his daughter as the lift zoomed up and up.

'It's all right, Papa,' the girl whispered to her father.

'Which ward do you want?' the palagi asked.

'Nine, please,' replied the man.

'Have you got someone there?' asked the palagi.

'Yes, my wife.'

'Oh, what's he saying, Papa?' the girl interrupted. She didn't understand English.

'He's just talking about the weather,' he lied to her.

'Sure wish I could speak their tongue,' she said. The palagi smiled at her. She blushed. Her father laughed with the palagi.

The lift halted and they nearly fell to the floor. The girl laughed shrilly.

'Here it is,' said the palagi.

'Thank you,' said the man as he stepped out, followed by his daughter.

'She's jake,' called the palagi. 'Hope your wife is well.' The door of the lift closed and continued up.

The girl felt her father's hand trembling, and she asked with concern: 'Did he upset you, Papa? What did he say?'

'Nothing,' he murmured, avoiding her eyes.

They waded through harsh neon light down the metal corridor towards the door of ward nine, where they paused, afraid to enter.

'C'mon, Papa,' the girl said to her father, 'Mamma's in there.' She pushed open the door and pulled him in after her.

They halted, confronted by an alien world full of white sheets and rows of distorted beds burdened with women patients who stared at them blank-faced like interrogators. The girl heard someone moan. She looked up. A parched woman with an enormous belly lay writhing, connected by a thin rubber tube to a hanging bottle of blood. She stifled a scream and huddled closer to her father.

'Where's Mamma?' she asked. He tried to look for her, but couldn't find her.

A frail-looking nurse, immaculately dressed in a white uniform, hurried to them, her face fixed in an official smile.

'Hallo,' she greeted them, bending down and smiling at the little girl, who stepped behind her father's legs and peered at her. 'What can I do for you?' But before he could answer she said, 'Oh, come with me.' The smile had vanished from her face.

The man and his daughter followed her down the aisle, staring straight ahead, afraid to examine the world of suffering around them.

The nurse paused in front of a door, tapped, opened it, and beckoned them to follow.

The room was in darkness.

The nurse slid open the curtains and a feeble light filtered into the room. The man and his daughter stood silently, staring at the figure on the bed.

'It is very . . . pain . . . very pain,' a weak voice murmured, cutting open the silence in the room. The nurse tiptoed to the bed and clasped the thin hand which the figure on the bed had extended to her. The nurse stared at the man and the little girl, not knowing what to do.

'Filemu,' the nurse whispered to the woman on the bed, 'your husband and daughter are here to see you.'

The woman gasped, and said: 'Come closer.' The man stumbled towards the bed, bent down, and kissed his wife. The little girl remained where she was, clutching the bunch of roses.

'You've brought her with you,' the woman said. Her husband nodded his head woodenly. 'You shouldn't have. I don't want her to see me like this.' Her voice broke. There was a strained pause.

'Are these for your mother?' the nurse asked the little girl, pointing at the roses. The girl didn't understand. She turned and ran toward her mother.

'Mamma! Mamma!' she cried, jumping up on to the bed and embracing her mother. The woman's arms clamped hard around her, wanting never to let her go. The woman wept. The child didn't know why. The man stood watching them; then he turned and gazed out the window.

'Look, Mamma,' said the little girl, 'I brought you some roses. You like them, Mamma? Eh? You like them?' The woman reached up and gathered her again into her arms. 'Mamma, will you be well soon? I want to show you round Auckland. It's big, Mamma. It's bigger than Apia and bigger than anything. . . .' Her voice raced on and on in a flood of impressions and memories for she had not seen her mother for two months.

'Emi, Mamma wants to rest now,' her father interrupted her.

'No, let her talk,' said his wife. And the little girl continued.

'Why are you crying, Mamma?' asked the girl. The woman shook her head and mumbled: 'I'm not, Emi.'

The child stopped talking, noticing for the first time how thin and fragile her mother had become. Then she buried her face in her mother's neck.

'You'll never leave me, will you, Mamma?' she asked.

'I want to talk to your father now,' said the woman, changing the subject.

'You go with Jane and have those roses put in a vase for me.'

Obediently the girl sprang down and took the nurse's hand, and they hurried to the door.

'You won't go away, eh, Mamma?' the child called from the door.

'No, Emi, I'll be here when you come back,' answered the woman.

The man came over from the window, sat down near the bed, and held his wife's hand.

'Will you tell her?' asked his wife. 'Or shall I?'

The man sat with bowed head. 'Do what you want. . . . I think she senses it already,' he said. His voice choked and they remained silent for a while.

Outside the storm whipped the city; and a man died under the wheels of a car.

The man remembered. The ten years of their married life buckled into one painful instant of time in his mind. And he felt guilt bite deep, ready to burst out like a silent scream.

'Forgive me, Filemu,' he sobbed, avoiding her eyes. 'Forgive me.'

'For what, Falesa? For what? You have been good to me.' She paused, turned his face to her, and, smiling, she kissed him. 'Yes, Falesa, you have been good to me. . . . I only hope I have been good to you.'

'Filemu,' he said, 'you have been good to me.' He stopped and wept. She reached down and, carressing his head, recited:

> *My flower, my garland of gold,*
> *The precious stone that was found;*
> *The bond of love grew strong between us.*
> *My life, my lily of the forest,*
> *The silver spring that was hidden;*
> *We penetrated illusion and found ourselves.*
> *And now till words decay; till . . . .*

She stopped abruptly and her husband sat up as the door flew open and their daughter and the nurse burst laughing into the room.

'How do you like that, Mamma?' asked the little girl, placing the vase of roses on the table next to the bed.

'It's nice, Emi, thank you,' replied her mother.

'Papa? Can you tell Jane thank you for me?' requested the girl, reaching over and clasping the nurse's hand. Her father spoke to the nurse in English. The nurse knelt down and kissed the little girl, then sprang up and fled from the room.

'Where's Papa going?' the little girl asked her mother as her father walked to the door and went out.

'He's going to see the doctor,' her mother lied.

'Is the doctor going to make you well, Mamma?'

'Yes . . . I think so.' She reached over and embraced her daughter.

'You smell funny, Mamma,' exclaimed the girl, 'but I like it.' Her mother laughed. 'Mamma, do you know, I smacked Edgar this morning because he pulled my hair. He cried, Mamma.

He's a cry-baby.' The woman chuckled. 'None of Auntie's children are as good as my brothers. They can't play hide-and-seek or anything like Sio and Loi. . . . They're sissies, Mamma.'

'They've been here a long time. They've forgotten how,' said her mother.

'Mamma, can we go home soon and see Sio and Loi?' the little girl asked.

'That's what . . . what I wanted to talk to you about, Emi,' began her mother. 'I mightn't be able to come back with you and Papa. . . . You see I have to stay and get well, so I can come home and see you and your brothers again. . . .'

'Good,' interrupted the girl. 'When are we going back?'

'I mightn't be, Emi; you might have to go back with Papa.' The girl's face fell in disappointment.

'Emi, do you remember your grandmother?' asked her mother.

'Yes, Mamma. Grandmother's gone with the Dark Angel, and she's in heaven now,' the girl replied quickly. 'You won't be going away like Granny, will you, Mamma?'

'That's what I wanted to tell you,' replied the woman, encouraged by her daughter's reply. 'You see, the Dark Angel may be coming for me like He came for Granny. . . .' She stopped, unable to continue.

'Do you want to go with Him, Mamma?' The woman didn't answer; she turned her face away from her daughter.

The door opened and the man entered. He looked at them, saw that his wife was weeping, and said, 'Emi, say goodbye to Mamma now. We have to go.'

The little girl kissed her mother and ran out of the room.

'Goodbye!' called her mother feebly; then she broke down and cried. The man embraced her. 'Don't bring her again, please. I can't bear it any more,' she sobbed.

He kissed her, turned, and walked slowly out of the room.

He found his daughter staring at the storm outside through a large window. He didn't know if she was suffering, if her mother had told her. The girl glanced at her father, and then again at the storm, fascinated. He walked over, took her hand, and led her down the corridor.

The tall figure of a palagi priest wearing a black soutane loomed ominously over them, as proud as a king. The child started and pressed to her father's legs.

'Good evening, Father,' the man greeted the priest, who stopped and returned his greeting.

'And how is she feeling this afternoon?' asked the priest in a deep voice which echoed and re-echoed in the corridor.

'Still the same,' replied the man, 'there's no . . . .'

'I know; the doctor told me as I came in. . . . I don't know what to say.' The priest placed his hand on the man's shoulder. The man felt soft inside, ready to weep, but he didn't want to in front of the child, who hid behind his legs, afraid of the priest.

The priest reached down and ruffled the girl's hair. She squirmed automatically away from his hand and glared up at him.

'Papa,' she whispered to her father in Samoan, 'let's go.'

'Thank you, Father,' the man said. He turned and led his child down the empty corridor.

'Papa,' asked the girl, 'was that the Dark Angel?'

'The Dark Angel?' replied the man, puzzled.

'Yes, Mamma told me that the Dark Angel might be coming for her like He came for Granny. . . . He's the Dark Angel, isn't He, Papa?'

'No, Emi. He's a man of God who has come to pray with your mother,' he replied.

'But isn't it God who sends the Dark Angel, Papa?'

'Yes, but a priest isn't the Dark Angel,' he said, doubting even his own answer.

The girl remained silent for a while. Then she asked, 'God isn't going to send Him for Mamma, is He? Because, if He does, I won't have a mother, and neither will Sio or Loi.'

'There are things we can't explain, Emi. Things which God alone knows the answers to,' was the only reply he could give her. He picked her up, embraced her, and carried her down the concrete stairs that spiralled down to the entrance and the city outside.

'I hope that man doesn't pray too long,' said the little girl.

'Why?' asked her father.

''Cause Mother's tired and she wants to go to sleep,' she replied.

After a while the girl suddenly said, 'I hope Mother likes it in heaven. Hope she meets Granny.' She embraced him, burying her face in his coat. She had accepted. He caressed her head. And he cried, feeling light, comforted, the load gone from him.

The storm was still alive when they emerged from the hospital. But the west was opening with a purple glow.

The man headed for home with his daughter snug in his arms.

The Silk

JOY COWLEY

When Mr Blackie took bad again that autumn both he and Mrs Blackie knew that it was for the last time. For many weeks neither spoke of it; but the understanding was in their eyes as they watched each other through the days and nights. It was a look, not of sadness or despair, but of quiet resignation tempered with something else, an unnamed expression that is seen only in the old and the very young.

Their acceptance was apparent in other ways, too. Mrs Blackie no longer complained to the neighbours that the old lazy-bones was running her off her feet. Instead she waited on him tirelessly, stretching their pension over chicken and out-of-season fruits to tempt his appetite; and she guarded him so possessively that she even resented the twice-weekly visits from the district nurse. Mr Blackie, on the other hand, settled into bed as gently as dust. He had never been a man to dwell in the past, but now he spoke a great deal of their earlier days and surprised Mrs Blackie by recalling things which she, who claimed the better memory, had forgotten. Seldom did he talk of the present, and never in these weeks did he mention the future.

Then, on the morning of the first frost of winter, while Mrs Blackie was filling his hot water bottle, he sat up in bed, unaided, to see out the window. The inside of the glass was streaked with tears of condensation. Outside, the frost had made an oval frame of crystals through which he could see a row of houses and lawns laid out in front of them, like white carpets.

'The ground will be hard,' he said at last. 'Hard as nails.'

Mrs Blackie looked up quickly. 'Not yet,' she said.

'Pretty soon, I think.' His smile was apologetic.

She slapped the hot water bottle into its cover and tested it against her cheek. 'Lie down or you'll get a chill,' she said.

Obediently, he dropped back against the pillow, but as she moved about him, putting the hot water bottle at his feet, straightening the quilt, he stared at the frozen patch of window.

'Amy, you'll get a double plot, won't you?' he said. 'I wouldn't rest easy thinking you were going to sleep by someone else.'

'What a thing to say!' The corner of her mouth twitched. 'As if I would.'

'It was your idea to buy single beds,' he said accusingly.

'Oh Herb—' She looked at the window, away again. 'We'll have a double plot,' she said. For a second or two she hesitated by his bed, then she sat beside his feet, her hands placed one on top of the other in her lap, in a pose that she always adopted when she had something important to say. She cleared her throat.

'You know, I've been thinking on and off about the silk.'

'The silk?' He turned his head towards her.

'I want to use it for your laying out pyjamas.'

'No Amy,' he said. 'Not the silk. That was your wedding present, the only thing I brought back with me.'

'What would I do with it now?' she said. When he didn't answer, she got up, opened the wardrobe door and took the camphorwood box from the shelf where she kept her hats. 'All these years and us not daring to take a scissors to it. We should use it sometime.'

'Not on me,' he said.

'I've been thinking about your pyjamas.' She fitted a key into the brass lock. 'It'd be just right.'

'A right waste, you mean,' he said. But there was no protest in his voice. In fact, it had lifted with a childish eagerness. He watched her hands as she opened the box and folded back layers of white tissue paper. Beneath them lay the blue of the silk. There was a reverent silence as she took it out and spread it under the light.

'Makes the whole room look different, doesn't it?' he said. 'I nearly forgot it looked like this.' His hands struggled free of the sheet and moved agross the quilt. Gently, she picked up the blue material and poured it over his fingers.

'Aah,' he breathed, bringing it closer to his eyes. 'All the way from China.' He smiled. 'Not once did I let it out of me sight. You know that, Amy? There were those on board as would have pinched it quick as that. I kept it pinned round me middle.'

'You told me,' she said.

He rubbed the silk against the stubble of his chin. 'It's the birds that take your eye,' he said.

'At first,' said Mrs Blackie. She ran her finger over one of the peacocks that strutted in the foreground of a continuous landscape. They were proud birds, irridescent blue, with silver threads in their tails. 'I used to like them best, but after a while you see much more, just as fine only smaller.' She pushed her glasses on to the bridge of her nose and leaned over the silk, her finger guiding her eyes over islands where waterfalls hung, eternally suspended, between pagodas and dark blue conifers, over flat lakes and tiny fishing boats, over mountains where the mists never lifted, and back again to a haughty peacock caught with one foot suspended over a rock. 'It's a work of art like you never see in this country,' she said.

Mr Blackie inhaled the scent of camphorwood. 'Don't cut it, Amy. It's too good for an old blighter like me.' He was begging her to contradict him.

'I'll get the pattern tomorrow,' she said.

The next day, while the district nurse was giving him his injection, she went down to the store and looked through a pile of pattern books. Appropriately, she choose a mandarin style with a high collar and piped cuffs and pockets. But Mr Blackie, who had all his life worn striped flannel in the conventional design, looked with suspicion at the pyjama pattern and the young man who posed so easily and shamelessly on the front of the packet.

'It's the sort them teddy bear boys have,' he said.

'Nonsense,' said Mrs Blackie.

'That's exactly what they are,' he growled. 'You're not laying me out in a lot of new-fangled nonsense.'

Mrs Blackie put her hands on her hips. 'You'll not have any say in the matter,' she said.

'Won't I just? I'll get up and fight—see if I don't.'

The muscles at the corner of her mouth twitched uncontrollably. 'All right, Herb, if you're so set against it—'

But now, having won the argument, he was happy. 'Get away with you, Amy. I'll get used to the idea.' He threw his lips back against his gums. 'Matter of fact, I like them fine. It's that nurse that done it. Blunt needle again.' He looked at the pattern. 'When d'you start?'

'Well—'

'This afternoon?'

'I suppose I could pin the pattern out after lunch.'

'Do it in here,' he said. 'Bring in your machine and pins and things and set them up so I can watch.'

She stood taller and tucked in her chin. 'I'm not using the machine,' she said with pride. 'Every stitch is going to be done by hand. My eyes mightn't be as good as they were once, mark you, but there's not a person on this earth can say I've lost my touch with a needle.'

His eyes closed in thought. 'How long?'

'Eh?'

'Till it's finished.'

She turned the pattern over in her hands. 'Oh—about three or four weeks. That is—if I keep at it.'

'No,' he said. 'Too long.'

'Oh Herb, you'd want a good job done, wouldn't you?' she pleaded.

'Amy—' Almost imperceptibly, he shook his head on the pillow.

'I can do the main seams on the machine,' she said, lowering her voice.

'How long?'

'A week,' she whispered.

When she took down the silk that afternoon, he insisted on an extra pillow in spite of the warning he'd had from the doctor about lying flat with his legs propped higher than his head and shoulders.

She plumped up the pillow from her own bed and put it behind his neck; then she unrolled her tape measure along his body, legs, arms, around his chest.

'I'll have to take them in a bit,' she said, making inch-high black figures on a piece of cardboard. She took the tissue paper pattern into the kitchen to iron it flat. When she came back, he was waiting, wide-eyed with anticipation and brighter, she thought, than he'd been for many weeks.

As she laid the silk out on her bed and started pinning down the first of the pattern pieces, he described with painstaking attempts at accuracy, the boat trip home, the stop at Hong Kong, and the merchant who had sold him the silk. 'Most of his stuff was rubbish,' he said. 'You wouldn't look twice at it. This was the only decent thing he had and even then he done me. You got to argue with these devils. Beat him down, they told me. But there was others as wanted that silk and if I hadn't made up me mind there and then I'd have lost it.' He squinted at her hands. 'What are you doing now? You just put that bit down.'

'It wasn't right,' she said, through lips closed on pins. 'I have to match it—like wallpaper.'

She lifted the pattern pieces many times before she was satisfied. Then it was evening and he was so tired that his breathing had become laboured. He no longer talked. His eyes were watering from hours of concentration; the drops spilled over his red lids and soaked into the pillow.

'Go to sleep,' she said. 'Enough's enough for one day.'

'I'll see you cut it out first,' he said.

'Let's leave it till the morning,' she said, and they both sensed her reluctance to put the scissors to the silk.

'Tonight,' he said.

'I'll make the tea first.'

'After,' he said.

She took the scissors from her sewing drawer and wiped them on her apron. Together they felt the pain as the blades met cleanly, almost without resistance, in that first cut. The silk would never again be the same. They were changing it, rearranging the pattern of fifty-odd years to form something new and unfamiliar. When she had cut out the first piece, she held it up, still pinned to the paper, and said, 'The back of the top.' Then she laid it on the dressing table and went on as quickly as she dared, for she knew that he would not rest until she had finished.

One by one the garment pieces left the body of silk. With each touch of the blades, threads sprang apart; mountains were divided, peacocks split from head to tail; waterfalls fell on either side of fraying edges. Eventually, there was nothing on the bed but a few shining snippets. Mrs Blackie picked them up and put them back in the camphorwood box, and covered the pyjama pieces on the dressing table with a cloth. Then she removed the extra pillow from Mr Blackie's bed and laid his head back in a comfortable position before she went into the kitchen to make the tea.

He was very tired the next morning but refused to sleep while she was working with the silk. She invented a number of excuses for putting it aside and leaving the room. He would sleep then, but never for long. No more than half an hour would pass and he would be calling her. She would find him lying awake and impatient for her to resume sewing.

In that day and the next, she did all the machine work. It was a tedious task, for first she tacked each seam by hand, matching the patterns in the weave so that the join was barely noticeable. Mr Blackie silently supervised every stitch. At times she would see him studying the silk with an expression that she still held in her memory. It was the look he'd given her in their courting days. She felt a prick of jealousy, not because she thought that he cared more for the silk than he did for her, but because he saw something in it that she didn't share. She never asked him what it was. At her age a body did not question these things or demand explanations. She would bend her head lower and concentrate her energy and attention into the narrow seam beneath the needle.

On the Friday afternoon, four days after she'd started the pyjamas, she finished the buttonholes and sewed on the buttons. She'd deliberately hurried the last of the hand sewing. In the four days, Mr Blackie had become weaker, and she knew that the sooner the pyjamas were completed and put back in the camphorwood box out of sight, the sooner he would take an interest in food and have the rest he needed.

She snipped the last thread and put the needle in its case. 'That's it, Herb,' she said, showing him her work.

He tried to raise his head. 'Bring them over here,' he said.

'Well—what do you think?' As she brought the pyjamas closer, his eyes relaxed and he smiled.

'Try them on?' he said.

She shook her head. 'I got the measurements,' she said. 'They'll be the right fit.'

'Better make sure,' he said.

She hesitated but could find no reason for her reluctance. 'All right,' she said, switching on both bars of the electric heater and drawing it closer to his bed. 'Just to make sure I've got the buttons right.'

She peeled back the bedclothes, took off his thick pyjamas and put on the silk. She stepped back to look at him.

'Well, even if I do say so myself, there's no one could have done a better job. I could move the top button over a fraction, but apart from that they're a perfect fit.'

He grinned. 'Light, aren't they?' He looked down the length of his body and wriggled his toes. 'All the way from China. Never let it out of me sight. Know that, Amy?'

'Do you like them?' she said.

He sucked his lips in over his gums to hide his pleasure. 'All right. A bit on the tight side.'

'They are not, and you know it,' Mrs Blackie snapped. 'Never give a body a bit of credit, would you? Here, put your hands down and I'll change you before you get a chill.'

He tightened his arms across his chest. 'You made a right good job, Amy. Think I'll keep them on a bit.'

'No.' She picked up his thick pyjamas.

'Why not?'

'Because you can't,' she said. 'It—it's disrespectful. And the nurse will be here soon.'

'Oh, get away with you, Amy.' He was too weak to resist further but as she changed him, he still possessed the silk with his eyes. 'Wonder who made it?'

Although she shrugged his question away, it brought to her a definite picture of a Chinese woman seated in front of a loom surrounded by blue and silver silkworms. The woman was dressed from a page in a geographic magazine, and except for the Oriental line of her eyelids, she looked like Mrs Blackie.

'D'you suppose there's places like that!' Mr Blackie asked.

She snatched up the pyjamas and put them in the box. 'You're the one that's been there,' she said briskly. 'Now settle down and rest or you'll be bad when the nurse arrives.'

The district nurse did not come that afternoon. Nor in the evening. It was at half-past three the following morning that her footsteps, echoed by the doctor's sounded along the gravel path.

Mrs Blackie was in the kitchen, waiting. She sat straight-backed and dry-eyed, her hands placed one on top of the other in the lap of her dressing gown.

'Mrs Blackie. I'm sorry—'

She ignored the nurse and turned to the doctor. 'He didn't say goodbye,' she said with an accusing look. 'Just before I phoned. His hand was over the side of the bed. I touched it. It was cold.'

The doctor nodded.

'No sound of any kind,' she said. 'He was good as gold last night.'

Again, the doctor nodded. He put his hand, briefly, on her shoulder, then went into the bedroom. Within a minute he returned, fastening his leather bag and murmuring sympathy.

Mrs Blackie sat still, catching isolated words. Expected. Peace-fully. Brave. They dropped upon her—neat, geometrical shapes that had no meaning.

'He didn't say goodbye.' She shook her head. 'Not a word.'

'But look, Mrs Blackie,' soothed the nurse. 'It was inevitable. You knew that. He couldn't have gone on—'

'I know, I know.' She turned away, irritated by their lack of understanding. 'He just might have said goodbye. That's all.'

The doctor took a white tablet from a phial and tried to persuade her to swallow it. She pushed it away; refused, too, the cup of tea that the district nurse poured and set in front of her. When they picked up their bags and went towards the bedroom, she followed them.

'In a few minutes,' the doctor said. 'If you'll leave us—'

'I'm getting his pyjamas,' she said. 'There's a button needs changing. I can do it now.'

As soon as she entered the room, she glanced at Mr Blackie's bed and noted that the doctor had pulled up the sheet. Quickly, she lifted the camphorwood box, took a needle, cotton, scissors, her spectacle case, and went back to the kitchen. Through the half-closed door she heard the nurse's voice, 'Poor old thing,' and she knew, instinctively, that they were not talking about her.

She sat down at the table to thread the needle. Her eyes were clear but her hands were so numb that for a long time they refused to work together. At last, the thread knotted, she opened the camphorwood box. The beauty of the silk was always unexpected. As she spread the pyjamas out on the table, it warmed her, caught her up and comforted her with the first positive feeling she'd had that morning. The silk was real. It was brought to life by the electric light above the table, so that every fold of the woven landscape moved. Trees swayed towards rippling water and peacocks danced with white fire in their tails. Even the tiny bridges—

Mrs Blackie took off her glasses, wiped them, put them on again. She leaned forward and traced her thumbnail over one bridge, then another. And another. She turned over the pyjama coat and closely examined the back. It was there, on every bridge; something she hadn't noticed before. She got up, and from the drawer where she kept her tablecloths, she took out her magnifying glass.

As the bridge in the pattern of the silk grew, the figure which had been no larger than an ant, became a man.

Mrs Blackie forgot about the button and the murmur of voices in the bedroom. She brought the magnifying glass nearer her eyes.

It was a man and he was standing with one arm outstretched, on the highest span between two islands. Mrs Blackie studied him for a long time, then she straightened up and smiled. Yes, he was waving. Or perhaps, she thought, he was beckoning to her.

The Liar

WITI IHIMAERA

You wouldn't believe, looking at me now, that once upon a time I was the fattest little boy in Waituhi. Lately I've become even thinner. My Pakeha friends are constantly saying, 'Henare! You're losing weight!' or 'Hey! You're looking slim.' And sometimes I look at myself in the mirror in my tweed jacket, quite loose now, and wonder where I am.

Mind you, I like being called slim, and it makes me feel as if I'm really handsome when I walk with Hone Wilson who's got a big puku. In fact I find I've started collecting fat people the way philatelists collect valuable stamps, except that my hobby is much easier—fat people aren't as rare.

The only trouble is that when I go home, back to Waituhi, my Maori friends, especially my relatives (who are so numerous that sometimes I've got to think: now that's Auntie Roha or is it Auntie Miriama or maybe it's Auntie Kaa) aren't nearly as overflowing with compliments. Instead of 'slim' I'm 'skinny' or 'bony'; and instead of looking 'healthy' I'm looking 'sick' or I've 'got Tb'. At home my mother tries to feed me up with huge steaming plates of kumara and puwha and pork. But my stomach's shrunk now. 'No thanks, Mum,' I have to say, 'I'll just have some yogurt.' 'Yogurt? What that stuff?' Mum asks. 'Sour milk,' I say. Then she really does her bun. 'What's wrong with sour milk?' I ask. 'You're always taking corn to the stream and leaving it there to get rotten before you eat it. Same thing.' 'But that's not all I eat,' she says.

But I really offended her last time I went home. She and Dad had gone out to Wainui to get some kina and mussels and she boiled them in a big pot. 'None for me, Mum,' I said to her, 'I'll just stick with my banana.' That was the last straw. She began to speak flat out in Maori, meta meta mea, on and on. She always growls at us kids in Maori when she's angry because she knows we don't understand. And she's too much a lady to swear in the English. Now I'm scared to go home for Christmas because I'm sure she'll see that I've lost another five pounds.

And my father's the same as Mum. Yet he started it all with that story he told me. When I say he's fat I mean he's really FAT. Over eighteen stone and can't even see his feet. When he goes out fencing I ask him, 'Shall I come and give you a hand?' But he looks at me and shakes his head and goes out to catch his horse without even answering me. I'm not very good at digging in fence posts anyway.

But, as I was saying, I was once the fattest boy in all of Waituhi. Pakeha would have called me 'plump' or 'chubby'; Maoris call you 'hinu' or 'puku hinu' or 'hapu' if you're so fat that you look pregnant. Maoris are too honest; they've got no Pakeha tact.

I was always eating. Three meals a day wasn't enough. And I loved doughboys, which are small balls of flour, usually eaten with puwha. I used to take seven pieces of porou rewana or Maori bread to school for lunch, topped with large chunks of butter and spread with jam. Strawberry was my favourite. And if there was any cold meat left over from the feed the night before I'd take that too, stuffing the meat in my mouth, fat and all. No wonder I didn't have a girl friend in primary school.

I was a big guts. As soon as the bus left us at our gate I'd run into the house and ransack the safe. Sometimes I'd even go and milk the cow just to get the thick top cream to spread over a piece of bread. Mmm! So I wasn't lazy really.

Dinner time was best though, except that we called it tea. I wish the Pakeha would make up his mind and stop correcting me when I say tea instead of dinner. Anyway, around about four Mum would come home from planting maize or sweet corn, or whatever Pakeha call it, and light the stove. Then she'd call out to my sisters, Katarina and Teria, to peel the spuds. Most of the time Teria did them because Katarina was always hiding, usually in the lav, where she used to sit and read her *True Confessions*. She was cunning!

So Teria would peel a big pot, and Mum would wash a cabbage, which I hate but would eat anyway, and I would cut up the meat and say: 'That one's mine,' because it was the biggest hunk. Afterwards Mum would set the table, sometimes with Maori bread, which is the best, or Pakeha bread, which isn't as good, lots of butter, a bottle of tomato sauce, and some Gregg's orange cordial. Then we'd sit and wait for tea to cook.

How I used to hate waiting for tea, I can tell you. Just painful sniffing how lovely was the kai. So I'd have a piece of bread or chew on a corncob or slurp away on a slice of water melon if it was summer. I never used to go away because I was scared that Dad would eat my tea. He was a big eater. Still is; that's why he's got a big puku.

Then Mum would shout out the window. 'Tom, Tom Tumata, come home!' And if he didn't whistle back, she'd have to call again. But Dad usually always heard her the first time, because he knew that if he was late for tea I'd eat his kai. In our house we never sat down together. Mum just left us in the kitchen and we helped ourselves from the pots on the stove. Mum couldn't stand the sight of us in the kitchen, our loud sucking noises. She'd learnt manners when she was a servant lady for the Andrews.

So Dad had to hurry up if he wanted tea. Because all us kids used to get stuck in and pile our plates full. In those days there was no Ladies First. It was First Come First Served. Anyway my sisters weren't ladies then. They are now, I hasten to add.

But even with the big lot that Mum used to cook I still never used to get full. Except for the times that Katarina and Teria went on a diet because they wanted to make a hit with some boy at school. But they didn't do that often. Stay on a diet, I mean. But even when they were dieting I suppose I wasn't really full. I couldn't have been, because straight afterwards my stomach would start to rumble and I'd have to eat something, anything.

Anyway there I'd be, getting stuck into the kai when Dad got home, trying to finish my plate before he got started. He was even worse than me. He'd run to the stove, still in his hobnail boots, shovel the kai on to his plate, and start eating before he even sat down.

We must have looked stupid really—the two of us, sitting at opposite ends of the table, glaring at one another between potatoes. We were enemies at tea time, throwing daggers at each other, and racing to see who got back to the pots first. If I had a good head start I used to win. But most times, I suppose, Dad beat me. He had a bigger mouth. Mum used to be really disgusted with us. Off she'd go in Maori, meta meta mea, shaking her finger at both of us. But we'd be too busy to listen. If you put your fork down and listened politely, like you have to do at a Pakeha home, you ended up staring at an empty pot. It's okay if you're Pakeha because you're usually not so hungry, even though you have to wait longer for tea. I mean dinner. But in our house Mum could never get a word in edgeways. She'd throw her hands up in despair, mumble. 'Titiro nga poaka!' (Look at the pigs!), and shuffle out before she really got sick. Poor Mum!

Well, looking back, I must have been a real pig all right. In fact I think that if we hadn't lived on a farm Dad would have been bankrupt by now, trying to feed us all, especially myself. But him too. I remember even that he said he put bets on the horses only because he was getting broke. And then he'd fix me with an angry look, as if I was to blame. But I wasn't, not all the time to blame. Him too.

I suppose things had to come to a head some time. And that some time came when Dad arrived back home from mustering to find I'd cleaned out all the pots. I knew I shouldn't have done it. But I was so hungry and I knew Dad wouldn't give me a hiding anyway. He went mad though, and clomped out to find Mum and tell her to make some more tea. Then he came back and watched me. I should have known he was up to something by the silly smile he had on. But I was too busy stuffing the last potato in my mouth, afraid that he might reach over and pinch it.

I finished the kai, and for good measure licked the plate. Then I leant back and sighed. I would have liked to burp but that was bad manners. So I let off a quiet fart instead, just a quiet one, so nobody would know it was me. I looked at Dad. I felt a little sorry I'd been such a pig because I knew I should have left him something. But that was his worry. Anyway I was surprised to see him smiling back. I should have known something was up. Dad's cunning.

'Good the kai?'

I nodded.

Then Dad told me the story which I now tell you. You must remember that I was a very impressionable boy in those days —would you believe it, I thought the stork story was true until I was thirteen? I tell you I must have been a real sucker. Not now though. I've grown up. Storks don't carry babies, no.

'You know Mangatu?' Dad began.

I nodded. Mangatu was a small village like ours in the same district. Lots of my friends came from there.

'Well,' Dad continued, 'I lived there once with my Auntie Ngaro for about a year. There used to be a pa there then. No flash motorcar, hardly any Pakeha around. Just the pa and all us Mangatu.'

Dad smiled. He knew I liked stories.

'I went to live with Auntie Ngaro when I was very small, about your age. Those was good times—no school, plenty of horses, lots of time to go swimming in the river. I had a lot of friends and we all used to go down to the willow tree and swing on a rope and let go and fall in the river. No clothes, just bare naked. I was skinny too.'

I wanted to laugh. I couldn't imagine my Dad without his pot belly.

'Anyway,' Dad continued, 'my best friends were Whiti and Uenuku, but I liked Whiti best. He was good, looked something like you, fat.'

He paused, remembering.

'Well, to get to the river we used to had to go past the pa. Every time we went for a swim, past the pa. And in the pa there used to be this old man called Hata. Old Hata. All the time he was there, sitting on the ground, about eighty-seven. He's dead a long time now. He used to had a moko and cloak and even a feather in his head. He was always there, sitting in the sun, mumbling to himself.

'But every time me and Whiti walked past, old Hata, he stops his talking to himself and looks up. A funny look he would give us, and his mouth it would start to water. We'd go past and I'd feel him looking after us, and I'd look back and see him shivering like he was cold.

'Every time he look at us as we go to the river and made me scared. There was funny stories about Hata.'

I looked at Dad, interested. I liked stories.

'Well, as I say,' Dad resumed, 'me and Whiti was good friends and we did everything together. But one day I had to do something or other for Auntie, and I told Whiti, "You go on down to the river. I'll come soon." So Whiti went. . . .

'And that was the last anyone saw him.'

I gasped.

'We searched for him all over the place and we called out: "Whiti! Whiti! Where you gone? Whiti! Whiti!" all night and all day for a long long time. But he was gone. Everybody says: "He must be drowned in the river," and we was all very sorry. So we had a tangi.'

Dad paused. He knew how to make a story good.

'But you know, son, I had a feeling that Whiti hadn't drowned. He was dead though, I was sure. How was I sure?

'Because I can still remember how Whiti was very fat, the fattest boy; and I still remember those funny stories they told about Hata.

'But most of all, I remember plain as day seeing Hata sitting in front of the pa the day Whiti got lost. He wasn't mumbling any more. No. He was just lying in the sun, his hands folded over his puku, licking his chops and smiling as if he'd just finished a big feed!'

And that's the story my father told me. For a moment I was stunned, especially since Dad was looking at me very solemnly. Because I was fat too like Whiti! I know I should have had more sense than to believe him; he was such a big liar. He's cunning, Dad is.

But I ask you—if you'd heard a story like that when you were small, wouldn't it put you off your feed?

No wonder I'm skinny.

The Child

WITI IHIMAERA

—Haere mai, mokopuna, she would say.

And always I would go with her, for I was both her keeper and her companion. I was a small boy; she was a child too, in an old woman's body.

—Where we going today, Nanny? I would ask. But I always knew.

—We go down to the sea, mokopuna, to the sea. . . .

Some people called my Nanny crazy, porangi. Whenever I heard that word, my heart would flutter as if a small bird was trapped in there and wanted to get out. My Nanny wasn't porangi, not to me.

But always, somebody would laugh at her and play with her feeble mind as if it was a kaitaka, a top which you whipped with flax to keep spinning. They would mimic her too, the sudden spasms that shook her body or the way she used to rock her head when her mind was wandering far away.

Dad, he told me that those people didn't understand or that they were only joking. But I'd see the sharp flints gleaming in their eyes and the cruel ways they lashed out at her. I would yell Stop! Don't you make fun of my Nanny. I used to hate them all.

I loved my Nanny. I would pat her on the head and hug her close to me. And she would whimper and put her arms around me too.

—Where my rahu, she would ask me. Where my rahu?

And I would help her look for it. I knew always that the basket would be under her bed, but Nanny, she liked playing pretend, so I'd play along with her.

—I don't know, Nanny, I'd tell her as we searched in all the dark corners of her room. Is it in the drawer? No, not there. In the wardrobe? No . . . might be in the corner, ay? No. Where you put it, Nanny? Where?

And all the time, she would answer me in a vague voice, just like a little girl.

—I don' know, mokopuna. I don' know where I put my rahu. It's somewhere. Somewhere here, somewhere. . . .

We'd play the game a little longer. Then I'd laugh.

—Here it is, Nanny! Here's your bag!

Her eyes would light up.

—You found it, mokopuna? You found my rahu? Ae, that's it, that my rahu.

I would put it in her hands.

—You ready to go now, Nanny? I'd ask. We go down to the sea now?

—I put my scarf on first, ay, she would answer. Might be cold, might be makariri. . . .

Those other people, they never saw my Nanny the way I did. And some of the kids at school they used to be funny to her. Willie Anderson, he would make faces and act all crazy. He would follow Nanny and imitate the way she walked. His father caught him once, and gave him a good hiding. But Willie didn't feel sorry; he only hated Nanny more. And he told lies about her. We had a fight after school one day. He was tougher than me and he won. But I didn't care, not even when he told some other kids I was porangi too.

I had my Nanny; I didn't need anybody else.

—You fullas just leave my Nanny alone, I told them. Don't you touch her even.

Willie, he just laughed and threw dust at me.

But he was only jealous, because he'd thought that when Nanny was staring in the sky, she was looking at nothing.

—No! I've seen what she looks at, Willie Anderson, I've seen her world. She's taken me there.

Willie didn't like that. He never liked being left out of things. That's why he was jealous.

—Come to me, Nanny, I would say.

And she would come and lift her head so that I could put her scarf on her. She would sit very still and very silent, and her lips would move without saying anything. The words were soundless.

—Yes, Nanny, I would answer. We're going down to the sea soon. Just wait your hurry. No don't say bad words to me. Nanny! I heard what you said that time! You're a bad girl!

My Nanny, she knew when I was angry with her. Her eyes would dim and she would fold her hands carefully in her lap. Sometimes, a small drop of spittle would trickle from her mouth.

—I'm sorry, mokopuna, she would whisper slowly.

I'd wipe her lips.

—Don't cry, Nanny. I was only playing. Don't be a crybaby, don't be a tangiweto!

And her eyes would light up, and deep down in them I'd see a little girl beginning to smile.

—You're cunning all right, Nanny! I would say. Those are only pretending tears! I know you, Nanny! So no more cry, ay? Come on, we go to the sea now. Haere mai.

And she'd put her hand in mine.

My Nanny, she used to be all right once. She never used to be porangi all the time. But when Nanny Pita died, something happened to her; I don't know what it was. Something. Perhaps it was because she found herself all alone and she was scared. Something.

I know she never used to be funny because Dad showed me some photos of her when she was young. She was pretty!

She used to be very slim and she had a shy way of smiling. Looking at her photos, you had the feeling that she wanted to tell you something, even after all these years. You waited for her lips to open, knowing that if they did, her words would be soft and beautiful.

But Nanny never spoke to me from her photos; she just kept smiling, and her lips curled around my heart and made it smile too.

—Where you going, Heta? Mum would ask.

And I would tell her, sometimes afraid that she might say, No, you and Nanny stay home.

—Me and Nanny, I would answer, we're going down to the beach for a little walk. Won't be long, Mum.

—Okay, but you look after Nanny, ay. If it gets cold, you put your jersey around her. If it starts to rain, you bring her home straight away. And don't get up to any mischief down there.

—All right, Mum.

And I would turn to my Nanny.

—Come on, Nanny. It's all right. Mum said we could go.

Come on, come to me, Nanny. Give me your hand. Don't be afraid.

And together, we'd walk out of the house.

Sometimes, my Nanny she'd be just like she was before Nanny Pita died, as if she was waking up from a long moe. She'd laugh and talk and her body wouldn't shiver all the time. But after a while, her mind would go to sleep again.

When she was asleep like that, I'd have to help her do things. Nanny couldn't even feed herself when her mind went away! —Come to me, Nanny, I would say. And she'd sit down, and I'd put a tea towel around her neck to stop the kai from getting on her dress. Open your mouth, Nanny. Wider yet. That's it. There we are! Wasn't that good? This kai's good ay! And she'd nod her head and make her moaning noises which meant she wanted some more. So I'd fill her spoon again, and she would smile to show she was happy.

—What that thing? Nanny would ask as we walked along the road.

And she would point to a house, a tree, a car or an animal grazing in a paddock. She liked pretending she didn't know what things were.

—That's a horse, that's a fowl, that's where Mrs Katene lives, that's a kowhai . . . I would tell her.

And she would repeat my words in a slow, sing-song voice. —A tree, a manuka, a fence, a horse. . . . No, that not a horse, that a hoiho, mokopuna.

—That's right, Nanny! I would say. You're cleverer than me, ay! You know all the Maori names; I don't, Nanny. Your mokopuna, he's dumb!

And she would giggle and do a little dance. Sometimes, she'd even sing me a song.

> *Tahi nei taru kino*
> *Mahi whaiaipo,*
> *Ke te wehenga*
> *Aroha kau ana. . . .*

And her quavering voice would lift its wings and circle softly in the air.

Nanny liked to sing. Sometimes, she'd be waiting at the door for me when I got home from school, and she'd have the guitar in her hands. Kepa, my brother, he gave me that guitar and learned me a few chords. But I didn't know how to play it proper. Nanny didn't mind, though. As long as I strummed it, she was happy. We'd sit on the verandah, she'd press my fingers to the strings, and as I played she would sing, one song after the other.

And sometimes, Dad would come and join us. 'What a racket!' he would say. 'Here, give that guitar to me.' And he would tune it and say to Nanny. 'Come on, Mum, we sing your song, ay? Ready, steady, go!' My Dad, he could play that guitar! And him and Nanny, they could sing as good as anything.

> *E puti puti koe, katoa hia. . . .*
> You're just a flower from an old bouquet,
> I've waited patiently for you, each day. . . .

That was Nanny's song. Her Pakeha name was Violet, and everybody called her that name because her Maori name was too long. And my Nanny, she was just like a violet; shy and small and hiding her face in her petals if the sun blazed too strong.

—We're almost there now, ay, mokopuna, Nanny would say.

And I would nod my head.

—Ae, Nanny. Almost there. Almost at the sea.

Nanny always said that same thing every time we reached the short cut to the beach. She'd hurry along the road to the gate. Beyond it, a path led through a paddock and down the cliff to where the sea was. Nanny, she would run a little ahead of me, then look back just to make sure I was following. She didn't like being alone.

—Haere mai, mokopuna! she would yell. Hurry up! The sea!

And she would cock her head to the wind and hear the waves murmuring. Then she'd run along a little further and flutter her hands at me to hurry.

I used to pretend not to hear her, and just dawdle along.

—Ay, Nanny? What you say? I would call.

And always, she would flutter her hands and lean her head into the wind.

My Nanny, she loved the sea. She and Nanny Pita used to live in a house right on the beach. But when Nanny Pita died, she came to live at our place because Dad was the eldest of her children. Dad, he told me that Nanny wasn't really porangi;

just old and lonely. He didn't know how long she'd stay with us because she was as old as Nanny Pita.

—You look after her and you love her, he said to me. Nanny, she might go away at any time. So while you have her, you love her, ay? I told him I would make Nanny so happy that she would never want to leave. But Dad, he didn't understand that I knew my Nanny wouldn't go away. He just smiled sadly and put his hands around my shoulders. Some day, he said. Some day. . . .

Sometimes, late at night, I'd hear Nanny crying because she was lonely. I'd creep softly down the corridor to her room and brush her tears away with my hands.

—You're too old to cry, I'd growl at her. But she'd keep weeping, so I'd hug her for a while. Turi turi, Nanny, I'd whisper. I'm here. Don't be afraid.

And sometimes, I'd stay with her until she went to sleep again.

—Here's one, mokopuna! she would yell. I got one!

And she would hold up a sea shell she had found.

My Nanny, she thought I liked shells; I don't know why. Maybe it was because when she first came to stay with us, she saw a paua shell in my room. Whatever it was, every time we went down to the sea, she'd wander along the beach, looking for shells to give to me.

—You want this one? she'd ask. And she'd cock her head to one side and look into my eyes. Sometimes, she looked so hard-case that I'd laugh.

—Okay, Nanny! We take it home.

Then she'd look very happy and drop the shell into her rahu.

—We taking you home, she would tell the shell. We taking you home for my mokopuna.

And every now and then, as we walked along the beach, she would let go of my hand to get another shell glittering on the sand.

—I already got enough, Nanny! I would yell.

But always, she would show it to me and cock her head as if she was asking a question.

—All right, Nanny, I would sigh. We take this one home too.

It used to be good just wandering along the beach with Nanny. If it was sunny and the sea wasn't rough, she'd let go of my hand more often, and wander off alone. I didn't mind, because I knew Nanny wasn't really alone; she was wandering with Nanny Pita on some remembered day.

But sometimes, a seagull would scream or cast its shadow over her head. Then she would stop and begin to tremble.

—It's all right, Nanny, I'd say. I'm here.

And she would reach out for my hand.

—You won't leave me will you, mokopuna? she would say.

—No, Nanny, I would answer. Turi turi now.

And we would walk together again. Nanny, she never left me when the sea was stormy. She used to be very scared and hold me very tight. Seaweed, it frightened her. She'd look at the waves and see the seaweed rising with them and whimper, afraid that she'd be caught by the long black fingers.

And sometimes, she would make me scared too.

—We go back home now, ay? I would ask her.

—Ae, we go home, mokopuna. Home. . . .

And she'd clutch her bag closely to her, and the shells would clink and scrape against each other.

One day, my Nanny, she wasn't home when I got back from school. I looked in her room, I looked everywhere, but I couldn't find her. Mum got worried and went to get Dad. But I knew where she'd be.

I ran down the road.

—Nanny! Nanny!

I don't know why I was crying. Perhaps it was because she had gone without waiting for me.

—Nanny! Nanny!

I heard the sea murmuring as I ran along the path, toward the cliff. I looked down to the beach.

My Nanny, she was lying there. . . .

—*Nanny!*

I rushed down the cliff toward her. I hugged her to me.

In her hand was a sea shell.

—Yes, Nanny, I said. That's a good one, that's the best one you've ever found for me. We put it in your bag, ay? We take it home. We go home now, we go home. . . .

But she didn't answer.

Her mind had wandered far away, and my Nanny, she had wandered after it.

—Haere mai, mokopuna, she would say.

And always I would go with her.

—Where we going, Nanny?

—We go down to the sea, mokopuna. To the sea. . . .

What Did You Do in the War, Daddy?

J. EDWARD BROWN

Lieutenant Vennel was an officer, I was only a corporal. That's the way it goes in wartime, but I did my best not to let him get too uppish.

I was never very happy in the army and Lieutenant Vennel didn't make it any happier. I couldn't escape him.

We first clashed when he was in charge at Suwarrow Island where we were coast-watching, radio operators—we were both dot-dash morse operators. There were no modern teleprinters where we were in World War II; communications were rather crude in those days, especially in peripheral areas.

When we first went there it was O.K. because we were civilians and Vennel was only Operator in Charge. But then alarm! Panic! The Japanese were sweeping all before them in their conquest of the Pacific and we received a message saying we had been conscripted into the army. We received an army number and a rank; corporal for me, lieutenant for Vennel, uniforms would be sent to us as soon as practicable but, as we didn't expect to see a boat until we were relieved in maybe a year or so, it was a laugh. The pathetic effort was a desperate attempt to give us status. If the Japanese had swept down we would have been spies in civilian clothes operating radio equipment behind enemy lines. And what the Japanese would say if they did come, and we produced a radio message saying we were in the army, I couldn't imagine—or more correctly I could imagine. They'd probably have taken the same action as they did at Tarawa and Betio—murdered us.

Lieutenant Vennel was the austere, ascetic, monkish type, and unadaptable. He might have risen to be prior of a monastery, but he'd never ever have made a beach-comber. He wasn't the type for such a life. He thought all local food was contaminated. He wouldn't even drink a coconut or eat a banana which are produced perfectly packaged by nature. He refused to eat anything that didn't come out of tins, yet the lagoon was alive with fish. We could get a full kerosene tin of crayfish from the reef in twenty minutes but he wouldn't touch them. So he lived on bully beef and baked beans. We operators got fat on the local tucker.

Lieutenant Vennel didn't drink either. We did—homebrew made from oranges. Great stuff, though we had to keep it hidden in a grove of ironwood trees, otherwise Lieutenant Vennel would have emptied it out and then murder would have been done. But that wouldn't have stopped him: he was that sort of bloke.

I hated him there on that island, but I had enough sense not to show it.

After a year of fighting boredom, and rust on our gear, we were relieved. I had a riotous week in Suva before being sent to Funafuti Island as a radio operator in the communications station. And I thought I'd seen the last of Lieutenant Vennel.

For the flight to Canton Island where I was to pick up a boat for Funafuti I removed my corporal stripes and pinned my hat badge on my collar, and the Yanks were too damned polite to ask what was my rank and what organisation did I belong to, and they treated me as an officer. I reckoned I should have been an officer—if it was good enough for Vennel, it was good enough for me.

I flew to Canton Island with an admiral and the first night I stayed in the officers' quarters as his special guest. But the next day Lieutenant Vennel appeared. I was promptly demoted to corporal and I was shifted in with the cooks. But they ate better than the officers—most of them were more intelligent too.

Lieutenant Vennel and I shipped out the next day on an old inter-island schooner for Funafuti. Lieutenant Vennel was as usual very rank-conscious; he slept below in a bunk in the saloon while I stretched out on deck. But all the crew slept on deck. Lieutenant Vennel was the only man below—and the most uncomfortable.

There was a District Officer of the Gilbert and Ellice Islands aboard. He and I drank whisky from his supply and swapped dirty stories and limericks. That D.O. was well educated. We had bet one shilling that we would finish each other's limericks

—you know the sort: 'There was a young lady from Funafuti.' And after hundreds of limericks I owed him only three bob.

The D.O. told me I should travel on to Christmas and Fanning Islands where he was to make a long overdue visit. The prospect was attractive, especially with the case of whisky he had, minus what we had drunk. But Lieutenant Vennel put the kibosh on that.

I had an argument with Lieutenant Vennel on board the ship in Funafuti lagoon. I refused to go ashore. I guess I had a hangover and I just couldn't stomach the thought of Lieutenant Vennel for an indefinite period on another island. If I was court martialled it would be a relief. I hated him with all the hate I could muster.

The old skipper saw my dilemma. I had got on very well with him; I got on very well with everybody—except Lieutenant Vennel. The skipper said, 'I know you don't want to go ashore with Lieutenant Vennel, but I'll order you to go ashore.' So that solved that.

Funafuti Island was garrisoned by a couple of hundred troops and after a year on Suwarrow in the Cook Islands it was almost civilised. But unlike the limerick there weren't any young ladies on Funafuti—there weren't any old ladies either.

The island has a huge lagoon with enough water inside it to float a fleet, which was why it was important. The natives had been cleared off our particular island and shifted to one of the other islands on the atoll.

I was on radio watch that first evening and I had a bottle of beer, purchased at great expense, in my quarters for supper. And I was really looking forward to it. But when I came off watch I couldn't find it. And the houseboy reported that Lieutenant Vennel had called in at our quarters on the way from his more palatial officers' quarters to the outdoor movies down at the other end of the island. So I knew what had happened to it.

I marched down to the theatre and had a notice flashed on to the screen: LT VENNEL PLEASE COME TO THE PROJECTION BOX.

He marched out, no doubt feeling very important.

'Where's my beer?' I demanded.

He accused me of insulting an officer.

I refused to apologise and he threatened to arrest me. We had heated words and I was marched away. I was hoping to be put back aboard the schooner but in the end I apologised—

it was not worth the loss of a week's pay for an officer like Lieutenant Vennel, and the schooner had sailed.

Then came the bull—not the army type. Cattle had been brought in by a plantation owner to graze under the coconut palms. The cows had all been knocked off by the Yanks and New Zealand troops on the island but this bull had gone wild.

I first saw it the night the bull attacked the radio shack. Lieutenant Vennel was in there with me, checking radio logs. I'd had my feet on the table when he'd come in, which hadn't gone down too well. Suddenly in the quiet of the evening something hit the side of the building with a thump like a shell landing, not that I'd ever seen or heard a shell land.

'We've been attacked,' Lieutenant Vennel shouted. 'The Japs. Send the attack signal.'

'Don't be bloody silly,' I said as the bull appeared in the doorway.

Lieutenant Vennel saw the bull and maybe the shock of it was worse than if the Japanese had landed. He went out through the window opposite like a circus star off a springboard.

Perhaps we should have ignored the bull, which charged a hut or a soldier only infrequently, but it seemed to have an attraction for the radio station. Perhaps it was the radio waves, but it would charge our building, get tangled in the feeder lines of our aerials and one night even knocked over an aerial.

Lieutenant Vennel was dead scared of it and was frightened to go out at night because he might be attacked. But when the bull one night attacked the verandah of his quarters and wrecked it, Lieutenant Vennel decided that something had to be done. He deputed me to shoot it.

'Why don't you do it yourself?' I said as rudely as I could.

'I am ordering you, corporal,' he said, drawing himself up.

Shooting had been my sport. I was looking forward to returning to New Zealand to do some serious shooting. I hadn't heard a shot fired in anger so far and it didn't appear as if I would.

It would be comparatively easy for anybody really determined to shoot this bull. The atoll islet we were on was long and narrow, a mile in length by maybe half a mile at its widest point. There was a wild overgrown taro swamp at one end of the island where the natives had cultivated a special atoll taro which would grow in brackish water, but it was a real jungle now. It was reckoned the bull had its hiding place in this overgrown swamp with taro plants higher than a man's head. And all we'd have to do was trap it there and shoot it.

I said that Lieutenant Vennel should accompany me. 'Lead me into battle. An officer's place is at the head of his troop,' I said—singular because there was only one of me.

He looked almost ill at the thought of it. But maybe he was braver than I thought because he agreed. He had acquired a revolver from somewhere now. 'That's not much good against a bull,' I said.

'You are the one who will shoot the bull,' he said coldly. 'I will provide the coup de grace.'

'A ceremonial execution.'

We had the help of Peni, a boy from the family who owned the animal, to track the bull. He had been brought over from one of the other islands. I shambled off down the beach with my .303—by this time I had been issued with a rifle. I could have shot Lieutenant Vennel in the back but I didn't really hate him that much, and Peni would probably report me.

'You sharp-shooter?' Peni said.

'No, radio-operator.'

'Radio operators no shoot.'

'This one does,' Lieutenant Vennel said, perhaps hopefully.

'Bull and taro very good,' Peni said.

'Whose bull?' I asked him.

'My uncle's.'

'If we shoot bull, no more little cows,' I said.

'We claim compensation from Americans,' Peni said. 'Bull shot in war. Then we buy newer bull. Lend-Lease.'

'You'll probably spend the money on beer,' Lieutenant Vennel said sourly.

Peni still remembered the Yanks. There were only New Zealanders on the atoll now and, as far as Peni was concerned, we were no substitute for the departed Yanks.

We marched northwards amongst the coconut trees, keeping a careful watch for the bull. But all we disturbed were island chickens.

'This will be something to tell your grandchildren, Lieutenant,' I said. 'How you went into action on a Pacific island.'

Lieutenant Vennel ignored me as he marched ahead.

'You like to buy grass skirt for your girl friend?' Peni asked Lieutenant Vennel.

'Lieutenant Vennel has no girl friends,' I said.

'Nobody has girl friends here,' Lieutenant Vennel said.

'But you have girl friend back home?'

I doubted it very much. I sometimes wondered if he'd ever had a mother. Maybe he'd come out of a can.

We came to the taro-patch area where thick growth choked the coconuts. It was a real jungle.

'My family pit,' Peni said.

We pushed our way through vines and trees. The flies were bad—don't let anybody tell you that South Pacific atolls are romantic. They've nothing but heat and flies. The best view of them is from the deck of a boat as you are leaving.

But the bull was there and was having trouble with the flies too. It stood in the shade of a taro plant shaking its head as the flies buzzed about it, having its afternoon doze in the tropical heat.

'An easy shot,' Lieutenant Vennel said, trying to hide behind a coconut tree and at the same time trying to appear brave—maybe something easy for Lieutenant Vennel: he'd been doing it all his life.

'Shoot,' Peni said.

The bull had its head in the air. The southeast trades were blowing at a steady fifteen knots and he was starting to get a whiff of us.

I leaned against the bole of the palm to steady the rifle.

Then the bull suddenly got wind of us and came out of the pit.

'Run!' Lieutenant Vennel said.

I took a shot, but missed.

Lieutenant Vennel was off out of the jungle heading for the beach. Peni was up a tree. I was up a tree too, but I couldn't emulate Peni. He was at the top of his, as far as he could go.

The bull was charging through the jungle like a miniature tank. It was debatable whether the bull or the lieutenant was making the most noise. This was war.

'New Zealanders very brave,' Peni shouted down. I don't know whether he was being sarcastic or not, he had done nothing to be proud of.

Then the bull broke free of the undergrowth.

I had a beautiful view from my high perch. The only one with a better eyeful was Peni, higher up a tree. The bull was chasing Lieutenant Vennel and Lieutenant Vennel was running like hell. No doubt he could hear the bull behind him.

The sand was soft and Lieutenant Vennel couldn't run very fast anyway—too much easy officer living. And the bull caught him and tossed him. And I'm not ashamed to admit I cheered.

Lieutenant Vennel landed in the water and commenced swimming even though the water was only six inches deep.

I held my breath. Would this be the end of Lieutenant Vennel? I hoped the bull would gore him. I don't know whether I was disappointed or not when the bull looked at him for a moment, almost contemptuously, and then turned away and ambled down the island.

I slid down and went to help Lieutenant Vennel. But he'd gone. He'd come out of the lagoon and raced off down the beach. By the deep marks he'd made in the sand he'd been in a real hurry. I followed the bull and eventually shot it.

I checked on Lieutenant Vennel, solicitously, in his quarters. He wasn't badly hurt, just a little wet. He didn't even ask what happened to the bull.

But he found out, eventually.

The remains stank to high heaven. You should have heard him rant and rave. I had shot the bull upwind from Lieutenant Vennel's quarters.

Peni refused to shift the bull and said nobody else could shift it either. He said it was sacred ground. It cost me a month's wages to bribe Peni to say that, but it was worth it. Peni called me Yank after that and Lieutenant Vennel never tumbled to it.

The shot that killed the bull was the only one I did hear fired in anger in the war—I was one of what was later called the chairborne brigade, fighting the battle of the overtime vouchers. Of course not many other troops saw much shooting. One of the passing Yanks at Funafuti reckoned he'd hit the beach at one invasion with the fifteenth wave—with the ice-cream machines and the mobile laundry.

Just the other day my boy said to me, 'And what did you do in the war, Daddy?'

After a pause I said, 'I shot a bull.'

And thinking of what I did to Lieutenant Vennel I don't know whether I was proud or not.

Holiday

PATRICIA GRACE

You know, I love my Nanny Retimana. Every holidays I say
to Mum and Daddy, 'I'm going to my Nanny Retimana's,'
and I pack my bag. And Mum and Daddy take me down to
the railway station and put me in the railcar, and even though
it's a long, long way to Nanny Retimana's place I don't care.
I wouldn't care if Nanny lived on the other side of the world
or up on the moon, I'd still go every holidays to see her.

Mum and Daddy put me in the railcar with some sandwiches and apples and comics, and they kiss me and tell me
everything to do and everything not to do. Then they kiss me
again and wave. And it is a little bit sad to go away from
Mum and Daddy, especially when they worry and keep telling
me this and that. But they shouldn't worry because I'm so happy
to go to Nanny Retimana's and I know everything to do and
everything not to do. And all the way in the railcar my Nanny
Retimana's name keeps going round and round in my head like
music—Nanny Retimana, Nanny Retimana. And Papa Retimana too of course. I love him too even though he cheeks me
a lot.

Nanny and Papa have an old car, and Papa won't let
anyone drive it but him. He goes everywhere in his old car. To
town, to the pub, to football; to Wellington, Auckland, anywhere. One day he even went over the bank in it, with Nanny
and my two Aunties and Uncle Charlie, all the shopping and his
beer and me. Roll, roll, bang the car went, and landed on its side
on the creek road below the bank. And I was sitting on top of
Auntie Materoa who was on top of Uncle Charlie who has a
stiff leg. I was glad I wasn't underneath because you should see
how fat Auntie Materoa and Uncle Charlie are.

None of us was hurt very much, but the eggs were all smashed and Papa Retimana got hit on the back of the neck with a tin of golden syrup. And Auntie Kiri was all spooky because the bag of flour broke and she had white eyebrows and eyelashes and a white chin. And she was sneezing all the time.

We all had to climb up out of the window, which was a tight squeeze for everyone but me, and Uncle Charlie couldn't get out at all because of his stiff leg. So Auntie Kiri had to get back in and push him up while the others pulled. Auntie Kiri was still sneezing too, and it took a long time to get Uncle Charlie out.

Gee, and the car was all dented and the shopping was everywhere. Eggs, flour, rolled oats, potatoes. Everywhere. But, you know, Papa's beer was all right. Not one bottle was broken and Papa was really happy. Auntie Kiri looked at the beer and she looked at Papa's happy face and said, 'E ta! The devil looks after his own. Hard case all right.' But Papa didn't care about her teasing because he was so glad about his beer.

Nanny and Papa Retimana always come down in their car to meet me at the station. I watch out the window and I see the two of them there and I'm glad because they look just the same as ever. I get out of the railcar and I go and hug them both, and you know, Papa Retimana nearly breaks all my bones with his big hug. I ride all the way back to Nanny's place squashed between my Nanny and Papa, and they say to me, 'Ah you still skinny Atareta,' and they shake their heads. And they say, 'Ah your mummy been cutting your hair,' and they shake their heads again. But I don't really think they mind how skinny I am. I don't think they're really angry about my short hair, they squeeze me all the way back to their place for thirty miles. And you know, my name isn't Atareta at all. My name's Lynette. But Nanny says I look just like my Auntie Atareta who lives way down the South Island and who I've never seen. And when my Auntie Atareta was little she used to sit on her legs with her feet sticking out at the sides the same as I do. Well that's what Nanny Retimana says, and Nanny Retimana, she calls me Atareta all the time.

When we come to Nanny and Papa's little house I see that it's just the same as the last time and I feel really glad. I like Nanny and Papa Retimana's house, all painted white with little paths running everywhere. The paths are all covered in stones and shells, and all the flower gardens are edged by big round river stones that Nanny and Papa have painted all colours. And it looks so cheerful always. I like arriving at Nanny and Papa's and seeing all the pretty paths and gardens, all the bright painted stones, and the little white house sitting in amongst it all.

When we get inside Nanny gets me a whole lot of kai out of the big pot on the stove so she can make me fat. And it's a wonder I'm not as fat as anything because I eat everything Nanny gives me, and I have bread and a big mug of tea as well. Papa cuts off thick slices of Nanny's bread for him and me. He puts thick butter on his bread and then he dips it in his tea. 'That's the way,' he says. 'Bread on butter and put it in the tea.' So I do it too and it's good, you know. It's a wonder I'm not as fat as anything.

After I've had my kai I go into Nanny's sitting room and look at all of her and Papa's photos.

'All your relations Atareta,' Nanny tells me. And she talks to me about all my old nannies who are dead now, and my aunties and uncles and cousins. There are photos of me there too with Mum and Daddy, and one of Mum and Daddy's wedding. And some of Auntie Atareta and her husband and kids who live way down the South Island. Some of the photos are hard case too, like the one of my cousin Danny pulling an ugly face, and the one of Uncle Charlie asleep out on the grass and all you can see in the photo is Uncle's big puku sticking up.

I'm always glad to go to bed after my long journey in the railcar, so after Nanny and I have looked at all the photos I change and get into my bed with the three mattresses on and go fast asleep.

Most days there's just Nanny and Papa and me, and I help them with the work and talk a lot. I help Nanny with the dishes and we polish the lino, and sometimes we make jam or bottle some fruit.

I like to go out and help Papa too. We feed all the ducks, and Papa's old pig, and his two dogs, and in the afternoons we often go out to the gardens and work there.

But in the weekends we have to be quick with our jobs because that's when all my aunties and uncles and cousins start turning up. And my aunties look at me and say, 'Ah that's you Atareta,' and they all kiss me and so do my uncles. Then all my cousins kiss me too, so it's no wonder I don't get fat after all because I'm sure I get worn out after a while. But I still like it. I like all my aunties and uncles and cousins coming.

And I get out and play with my cousins. We ride the horse

or go swimming in the river, or slide down the hills and wear
our pants out. We play all day long until dark, and when we
go back inside we're so hungry we eat everything out of the
big pot and all the bread as well. Nanny and Papa Retimana
and our aunties and uncles all have some beer and laugh a lot
and talk, and Auntie Materoa, well she can't stop laughing. She
laughs all the time. She sounds just like a fire engine with her
way of laughing. 'Eeee Hardcase, Hardcase, Eeeeee,' with tears
all running down. Uncle Ben teases her and says, 'You lay an
egg in a minute, Mattie.' And away Auntie Materoa goes again,
'Eeee Hardcase, Hardcase Eeeeee.'

Sometimes in the weekends instead of our aunties and uncles
coming, we get in the car and go to one of their places. I like
going to Auntie Kiri's place because it's not far from the beach.
And you know, Auntie Kiri's house is really neat. It's flash.
Auntie's place is all full of carpets and thick curtains and electric
heaters, and a big TV, a deep freeze, clothes drier, and stereo-
gram. Auntie's house is so flash she won't let us kids inside when
we've been out playing until we've had a good wash under the
hose.

We met Auntie in town one Friday and she told us to come
back and stay with them so we did. It was raining that day.
And when we got to Auntie's house Uncle Ben was sitting in
the kitchen and Auntie's big clothes drier was rumbling away in
the wash house. Auntie was really pleased with Uncle for doing
all her washing and putting it in the drier and she gave him a
big kiss.

Then afterwards she went to get the clothes out and she
started yelling her head off out in the wash house.

'Parengo. Your stink parengo! Who told you to put your
haunga seaweed in my drier?'

And Uncle said, 'How else do I dry my parengo in this
weather?'

And we all ran out to the wash house to look at Uncle's
parengo in Auntie's drier. Auntie Materoa who was there too
started up laughing as usual, 'Eeee Hardcase, Parengo Eeeeee,'
screeching, looking into Auntie Kiri's drier.

Gee, Auntie Kiri growled. She called Uncle a stink and a dead
loss and a taurekareka. Then after a while she started up laughing too, and Auntie Kiri's laugh is nearly as bad as Auntie
Materoa's, well that's what I think.

Auntie Kiri can growl you know. She doesn't growl at us
little kids though, only if we mess up her house, but she growls

at her big grown up kids, my big married cousins. They always come there and start looking in the cupboards and all round the house for Auntie's bread.

'You made a bread, Mum?' they say.

'You got any meat? Gee-ee, Macky forgot to get us a meat for the weekend.' And Auntie Kiri growls.

'Don't you come here looking for bread and meat you tahae things,' she growls. But I don't think she means it really because afterwards she goes and gets the bread from a tin in her wardrobe and we all have some. And my big cousins all grin and say, 'Gee what a lovely bread, Mum. Cunning all right.' And Auntie Kiri looks pleased and says, 'Cunning yourself.'

She growls too if they come to her place untidy. Mostly my cousins make sure to change before they come to Auntie's, but one day Benjy came in his old kanukanu pants and Auntie went off at him.

'Haven't you got a decent pants?' she said. 'Can't that fat wife of yours sew a button on your pants. Where is she anyway? At home with her eyes on the TV the lazy. You bring your wife next time, and bring my mokopuna. You didn't bring my mokopuna to see me.'

Then Auntie made a funny noise at Benjy to show how bad he was. 'A-ack!'

Later that night when I was pretending to be asleep on the settee I heard Auntie saying, 'Come here useless,' to Benjy, and I peeped through my eyelashes and saw her with a needle and cotton and a button, and she started sewing a button on my big cousin's pants. And Benjy was dancing up and down saying, 'Gee-ee, look out Mum. Watch out you'll sew up my thing in a minute.' Rude, ay?

But Auntie just said, 'Good job too,' and kept on sewing.

And of course Auntie Materoa started up screeching again. You know Auntie Materoa's hardcase with her laugh. I had to wriggle down under my blanket so no one would see my mouth grinning.

I like going to Auntie Materoa's too. I don't sleep on the settee at Auntie Materoa's, I just get in bed with all her kids. My cousins and I get up to all sorts at Auntie Materoa's. We have pillow fights, and use the beds for trampolines, and dress up in Auntie Materoa's clothes and put her shoes on. Four of us can fit in one of Auntie Materoa's dresses, that's how fat Auntie Materoa is. And nobody growls. Nobody takes any notice of us kids yelling and jumping around in the bedroom. Even when we sneak out in the kitchen and have a feed they take no notice at all. They all sit around in Auntie Mateora's sitting room and drink their beer and sing. And they dance and do the hula, even my Nanny Retimana who is quite old really. She does the hula and they all shout hardcase things to her like,

'Good on you aunt.'

'Swing it kuia.'

'Watch out, ka makare to tarau,' and that's just about rude because it means Nanny might lose her pants if she does the hula too much.

Nanny Retimana doesn't care, she shouts out, 'Shut up you fullas jealous, *E puru tai tama. . . .*'

They all sing *E puru tai tama,* and start clapping and sometimes Uncle Charlie gets up and joins in the hula, and that sets Auntie Materoa off again because Uncle Charlie's got a stiff leg, 'Hardcase! Hardcase!' tears running down and us kids all looking round the door to watch Uncle Charlie and Nanny Retimana and some others doing the hula.

I enjoy myself at my Auntie Kiri's and Auntie Materoa's, but I'm always pleased to get back to Nanny's where we can be peaceful and quiet again, and I go round helping Nanny and Papa and play with the ducks and Papa's two dogs, or have a quiet ride on the horse.

And my holiday never seems very long. It's soon time to pack my bag again and get into Papa Retimana's old car—it's still got all the dents in too and there's a stain on the seat where all the syrup poured out—and Nanny and Papa take me to the station and put me in the railcar with some kai in a biscuit tin, and some pauas in a plastic bag from Auntie Kiri to take home to Mum and Daddy.

I wave to my Nanny and Papa Retimana out of the railcar window. I wave and wave until I can't see them any more, and I'm sorry to be going away from them. Then after a while I start thinking about Mum and Daddy waiting for me at the other end, but it seems a long, long way. I have a few sleeps, and I nibble at all the kai Nanny Retimana has packed for me. Then as I get nearer to home I start to feel excited because Mum and Daddy will be waiting at the station for me. Then I think what if they've changed? What if they're different or don't know me? And I worry and put my face to the window as the railcar comes in, and I see them both standing on the platform waiting for me. And I see they haven't changed.

They're not different at all, and they do know me because they start smiling when they see my face at the window.

You know, I love Mum and Daddy. I pick up my bag and my tin of kai and my pauas in a plastic bag from Auntie Kiri, and I hurry out of the railcar and on to the platform. I hug Mum and Daddy and we go and get into our car. I sit between them on the front seat and they squeeze me all the way home to our place.

A Glorious Morning, Comrade

MAURICE GEE

Mercy tied her father's scarf in a mean granny knot.

'Now remember, darling, if you want the little house just bang on the wall. We don't want any wets with the girls all here.' And Barbie, gentler, but not to be outdone, knelt and zipped up his slippers. 'You'll be lovely and warm in the sun, won't you? Just bang on the wall. No little accidents please. 'Bye daddums.'

They left him in his rocking chair on the veranda and he rocked a little, pitying their innocence. He did not mean to pee in his pants today. He had other plans.

Presently the 'girls' came, driving their little cars; and they walked up the path in twos and threes, dumpy women or stringy, the lot, in Saturday clothes and coloured hair. They stopped for a little chat of course, politely, and sniffed behind their hands to see if he had behaved himself today. They were good-hearted women. Mercy and Barbie attracted such.

'Lucky you, Mr Pitt-Rimmer. Just loafing in the sun.'

He counted them. Ten. Three tables. There was Madge Ogden, a daughter of divorcees; and Pearl Edwards who taught mathematics at the Girls' High School; and Mary Rendt who had wanted to be a nun but had lost her faith and married a German Christian Scientist and lost that faith and her husband too; and the three Bailey girls, with not a husband amongst them, whose mother had broken their hearts by choosing to live in an old people's home; and Christine Hunt who had been caught shoplifting when she was a girl and lived it down and married the son of the mayor; and Jean Murray-Briggs, whose name annoyed him; and last the lesbians, though none of the others knew—Phyllis Wedderburn and Margaret Way. Charles

Pitt-Rimmer, he knew. He winked at them and they blushed, but seemed a little pleased.

'Such lovely sun. We've only got old bridge.'

He gave them time to get warmed up. Mercy looked out once and wagged her finger, and Barbie once and kissed him on the cheek.

They would forget him when they were well ahead. His daughters were the top pair in the district and he wished he could feel more pleased with them for it.

When the time came he stood up and walked along the veranda. He went down the path, down the steps, along the footpath to the park, and into the trees. It was twenty-nine minutes past two. He had run away twice before. Today he would outfox them. He would keep away from roads and butcher shops, where he had been caught twice before looking at roasts of beef. They would not think of searching on the hill.

Girls, he wrote in his mind, *There are other things than meat. Your father played chess.*

At nineteen minutes to three he reached the dairy. 'Here you children out of my way,' he said, and they stood aside with a quickness that pleased him. He did not mind that they giggled. That was proper in children.

'A bag of Turkish delight,' he said. He had planned it all morning and it came out with an English sound. 'And a packet of cigarettes.'

The woman behind the counter had a half-witted face, a nose that seemed to snuffle for scent like a dog's. She gave a smile and said, 'It's Mr Pitt-Rimmer, isn't it?'

'My name is not your concern. Turkish delight, and a packet of cigarettes.'

'Sit down, Mr Pitt-Rimmer. There's a chair right there. As soon as I've served these kiddies I'll ring Mrs Parsloe.'

'You will not ring Mrs Parsley. I wish to be served. Am I a customer or am I not? And are you in business? Answer me that.'

He was pleased to see confusion in her eyes. 'I'll have de Reszke.'

'Whosie?'

'De Reszke. You don't seem to know your business, madam. Do you make a living? I wonder at it.'

'There's nothing here called de Reszke.'

'Cigarettes. Cigarettes. Named after a great operatic tenor.

Before your time, of course. I understand. It's all Bing Crosby today.'

The woman went suddenly to the telephone. 'You kiddies wait.' She started to dial.

'Very well,' cried Charles Pitt-Rimmer. 'You may ring Mrs Parsley. Tell her I'm striking out. I have my life. Tell her I'm smoking again. De Reszke. And eating Turkish delight.' He stopped at the door. 'And if she wishes to know where I am you may say that I've gone to the butcher's for a piece of German sausage.'

'Mrs Parsloe?' the woman said. 'It's the Regal dairy. Your father's here.'

He was very pleased with himself as he turned up the hill. Capablanca would have been proud of that move.

Girls, bridge is for simple folk. You must think ahead. I've never cared for German sausage.

He looked at his watch. It was thirteen minutes to three. Already he had beaten his old record. He pictured the little cars scuttling about Hardinge, driven in a dangerous manner by women with blue and pink hair. Barbie would be crying—he was sorry about that—and Mercy with her eye like a hanging judge's.

Girls, a man's a man for a' that.

He followed a path into the trees and climbed until he stood on the edge of the cliff with the wharves below him. Three minutes past three. He would have liked some Turkish delight. He had not had any since his last day in court, which was twenty-two years ago. His secretary used to bring in a paper bag full with his lunch. The gob-stopper he'd taken from the Regal dairy's counter would be no substitute. But he found that he enjoyed it once he'd torn the paper off. It tasted of raspberry, a flavour he'd forgotten.

He went to the safety fence and looked down. A girl had jumped down there on Boxing Day because her employer, a well-known man in Hardinge, had put her in the family way. She had lived for two hours but not said a word. He had heard Mercy and Barbie discussing it, in voices hushed but full of glee and dread. The man, Barbie said, was 'a weed in the garden of life'—which she'd pinched from her mother, who had also believed that such men should be hanged. Women had a poor understanding of certain needs.

The gob-stopper made him feel bilious. He put it in his pocket. Below him ships were tied up at the wharves, all piddling water out of their sides. One of them was a phosphate tub, moored at a wharf that he remembered now was Pitt-Rimmer Wharf. There had been those years on the Harbour Board— a tedious business. Jack Hunt had picked his nose behind the agenda. The Hunts had never been up to much though they liked to believe that they were the bosses of Hardinge. He walked on and the cape came into sight, standing up like Chunuk Bair. He had no wish to be reminded of that. That had been a very great piece of nonsense.

Girls, you persist in reminding me. . . .

A woman came towards him leading a tiny black dog in a tartan jacket.

'I don't care for dogs, madam. Keep him off.'

'Mr Pitt-Rimmer. Don't you remember me?'

'I've met many people. Fifteen thousand is my calculation.'

'But I'm Maisie Transome. Maisie Jack that was. You used to give me lollies.'

'Your mother was an excellent secretary. And a kindly soul. She had extraordinary bosoms.'

'Ooh, Mr Pitt-Rimmer, you're a rogue.'

'I don't care for animals sniffing about my feet.'

'Come here, Bruce. Where are your manners, darling? Mr Pitt-Rimmer, can I walk home with you? You shouldn't be out you know, dressed like that. Barbie told me you're being very naughty.'

'My daughter has more kindness than sense. She's a good woman but she's had a tragic life.'

'Who? Barbie?'

'She fell in love with a young man in my office. Parsley was his name. Mercy stole him away. "Mercy" was not my choice. I want that understood. My wife had a poor grip on reality. But Parsley—she married him and broke her sister's heart. Barbie never married. Parsley was not a good catch, mind you. She was well out of it. He played around as they say. There was a woman in my office called Rona Jack. Her marriage was un-satisfactory. Parsley used to visit there.'

'Oh Mr Pitt-Rimmer—'

'He died of course. They nursed him. My daughters are good girls.'

'But my parents had an ideal marriage. They were in love till the day they died.'

'Indeed. I congratulate them. You should not speak with strangers. The risks are very great. Good day to you.'

'But I'm taking you home, remember?'

'I wish to relieve myself.'

She did not follow him though her dog yapped in an impertinent way. The path led downhill and had many troublesome curves. His legs began to be sore. But a bank of nasturtiums pleased him and a smell of fennnel. Fennel made him think of aniseed balls. He stopped at the memory. When sucked an aniseed ball turned white. And Turkish delight left sugar round the mouth.

Girls, when you were children I bought you sweets. Straps of licorice. Be fair. Bags of sherbert. Bags of chocolate fudge.

The path ended by the Salvation Army Eventide Home. Two old men were sitting on a bench. 'A glorious morning, comrade,' one of them said.

'Glorious,' Charles Pitt-Rimmer agreed, smiling at his better knowledge. It was twenty-nine minutes past three in the afternoon and his daughters were thoroughly bamboozled. He stopped by the reservoir and sat down on a bank. A boy was walking along a pipe, and a smaller boy rode up on a tricycle.

'Why are you wearing your dressing-gown?'

'Old men are allowed to.'

'Mummy makes me get dressed. Have you wet your pants?'

'I believe I have.'

'Couldn't you find a toilet? You could use ours.'

'The word is lavatory. You should not be frightened of calling things by their names.'

'Mummy said lavatory's not nice.'

'And you should not pay too much attention to women.'

Charles Pitt-Rimmer dozed for a moment. 'Poor Parsley. They made him eat his vegetables. Curly kale. A weed.'

'Mummy makes me eat my vegetables.'

'What do you have for pudding?'

His mind was lucid about food but cloudy about everything else. He was not quite sure where he was. 'My favourite is lemon meringue pie.' He felt in his pocket for the gob-stopper and gave it to the child who put it in his mouth at once, leaving only the stick poking out.

'You speak too much of your mother. The conspiracy starts at the cradle.'

The boy who had been walking on the pipe ran up to join them.

'Give us a lick, Tony. Come on.'

Charles Pitt-Rimmer went to sleep. He believed he was in a

bath of luke-warm water that was turning cold about his legs. Soon he was wakened by a woman's voice.

'Let me see that. Give it to me at once. It's filthy. It's got a hair on it.'

She moved her arm violently and the boy on the tricycle cried. Charles did not know what was happening, but he saw that the woman was looking at him with hatred and was astonished at the ease with which people felt this emotion. Forty years of court work had not got him used to it.

'Beware, madam. It can get to be a habit.'

'You ought to be ashamed of yourself. And you'—she rounded on the older boy—'I told you to look after him. Why can't you listen for once? Get into the wash house and wait till your father comes home.'

Now the older boy cried. They were an emotional family and seemed to be without reason, Charles decided. They vanished and he was relieved. He lay on the bank and tried to sleep, curled into a ball to defeat the cold. Where were his daughters? Where were the wretched women?

Girls, you're selfish creatures. . . .

Again a woman woke him. This time it was Christine Hunt, with her hair like candy floss. He reached out for some.

'What are you doing? Oh! Mr Pitt-Rimmer. Let go.'

'Christine Perkins, you were lucky to get off with a fine. If you hadn't had me to conduct your defence you would have gone to prison.'

'Oh! Oh! My hair. You've ruined it.'

'Why did you choose such frilly things, Christine? If you remember, I told the court they were for your glory box? A clever touch. But you can tell me. I can be discreet.'

'You're a horrible man. Oh, look, you've wet your pyjamas. This is dreadful.'

'I understand, Christine. It's difficult to be poor. No nice frillies, eh? A girl likes frillies. But I always believed you married beneath you. Your father-in-law picks his nose.'

'My father-in-law has been dead for twenty years. And you've ruined our afternoon. You know that, don't you? It's a wonder to me how Mercy and Barbie keep going. They must be saints.'

'They're vegetarians. They struggle to ward off despair. I do my best.'

'Mr Pitt-Rimmer, I'm going to take you home. I am. Now come with me. Come on.'

She put out her hand and he was appalled at the size of it. It went right around his wrist, and her silver nails poked up from the underside. She was appalled too. She jerked away.

'Barbie will be the invalid when I'm dead,' said Charles Pitt-Rimmer.

Christine Hunt went away. 'I'm going to get your daughters. Don't you move.' Her little car scuttled off, and Charles lay curled up tightly.

Girls, it's time for my nap. You're selfish creatures. . . .

'Oh daddums, daddums, why do you do these things?'

'Put down the rubber sheet, Barbie. No, spread it out, you ninny.'

They put him in the back seat and Barbie sat with him, rubbing his hands.

'You're so naughty, so naughty—'

'I've had enough,' Mercy cried. 'I'm going to put you in a home. You've made a fool of me for the last time. Wipe his mouth Barbie, can't you see?'

'You make it so hard for us, daddums. Oh, your hands are so cold.'

'I walked on the pipe, Mercy. If I'd fallen off you would never have been born.'

They washed him and put him to bed. He slept smiling for two hours, then rang his bell for tea. They propped him up with pillows, and Barbie sat with him while he ate. .

'It's a special salad, daddums. One Mercy found. It's got avocados in it. Now drink your apple juice.'

She took away the tray and came back with his library book.

'Promise me you won't be naughty again. It makes us so sad.'

'What was the time when you caught me?'

'Four o'clock. You were gone for two hours. Oh daddums—'

'An hour and thirty-one minutes.' He grinned at her.

When she had gone he finished his book. He corrected one split infinitive and underlined two mentions of female breasts. Then he made his secret sign on page eighty-eight.

Barbie was doing the dishes and Mercy watching a television show full of American voices. On the final page, below a scene of love, Charles wrote a message:

My daughters are keeping me prisoner. Help! I have not had a piece of meat for twenty years. . . .

King Bait

KERRY A. L. HULME

I think this season'll be the last, you know. Well, I mean,
Coasters have their channels for spreading news, mainly ex-
Coasters. From such people, news filters through to friends of
ex-Coasters, not to mention relations, and eventually travels the
length and breadth of the country. So maybe everybody knows
why, and maybe everybody doesn't yet.

Here I am, wound round in a welter of words, with a mystery
on my hands, and very uncertain what to say about it. But this
is the core of the matter, the heart of the nut: King Bait.

One thing everybody does know about the Coast is bait.
Whitebait. That succulent little fish, quick and lucent, likened
in an old haiku to the 'spirit of the waters'—

> *The whitebait:*
> *as though the spirit of waters*
> *were moving.*

And every beginning spring, Coasters in their hundreds flock
to the rivers and streams to swoop and scoop and blind-drag as
many as possible out of sanctuary. When it's a good season, tons
are lovingly packed into freezers against the lean, non-bait
portion of the year; tons more are railed and flown over the hill,
weekly. The Coast becomes a joyous place, the Coaster a con-
tented being.

Of course, quite a few hundred-weight get converted meantime into patties and omelettes and—well, whatevers. How did
your mother cook them when she got them from the shop? I'm
from Christchurch—we eke out the bait with flour and other
foreign bodies. But here! Prodigality. . . .

Take half a pound of bait per person, add an egg (two eggs, if you really like them), stir vigorously until fish and egg is a viscous froth full of strange little eyes. Add half a teaspoon of baking powder; a little salt; a smidgeon of pepper, and fry the mix quickly, but with care. There you have a Coast feed, two right-sized whitebait patties, a subtly flavoured delight for anyone with a tongue in their head.

Last year, I missed the whitebait season. I was newly arrived from Christchurch, and unaware of Coast ways, I bought my bait from a local fish-shop, and was well content to get it 40 cents cheaper the pound than the family over the Hill. Last year, I couldn't have told you the difference between a net for the Tere, and one used in the Grey. Nor what the advantages of supplejack over duraluminum. Set-nets were strangers, and the joys of very early morning tea in a tin shack on a river-side also unknown. The haiku was just a pleasant poetic fancy, blind-dragging was peculiar terminology and the great runs—well, myths of the past, a nice concept to beguile the tourists.

This year, I'm all enthusiasm. Buy myself the regulation round Grey net, and a bloody great pole to go with it. Equip myself with gumboots, get out old fishing clothes, and head down to the river at odd hours, waiting on changing tides. Drag that net, eyes strained, shoulders filled with a dead ache, hopeful of a nice little pudding in the bottom of the nylon bag. Or a very large one, for the season's started out a boomer. Tons of bait about. Happy faces all around, reflecting my smug grin. Full stomachs abounding, appetite satisfied, bankbook replete, and yet expecting much, much, more.

Things are just beginning. All over the Coast the hiss of hot fat and the crunching of little eyes. . . .

And you know what? I think it's the end.

A very strange thing happened yesterday, twenty to nine under Cobden bridge; a strange, a horrible, a holy thing.

Friday night was a good night. I'd been to the local juicery, talked a lot, sung a bit, drank to capacity, happy among happy people. Came home with the white moon high over the sea. A windless peace-filled night, the only sound that liquid continuous chirruping of tree-frogs. I cooked a couple of patties, ate them with a last cold beer from the fridge, and went to bed. Relaxed, full, content, perfectly at ease . . . ah, sweet.

And then, the morning. I woke suddenly, dropped abruptly out of sleep. For a moment I couldn't place the awakening factor, and then, there it was. A most peculiar hysterical liveness, filling the quiet street, streaking up my quiet hill, a shrill cacophony of voices.

'Berloody kids,' I think, and go to turn over, back to sleep. It penetrates then:

'Whitebait running WHITEBAIT RUNNING WHITE BAIT. . . .'

The words and the strangeness were enough. I shot out of bed, into my denims and t-shirt faster than it's said, grabbed my boots and the net, and screamed out of the door and down the hill far more quickly than I've ever done. In fact, I'd reached the bottom before I realised that I've left the pole back in the house. Or asked myself why somebody should tell everybody about a good thing.

But the street is alive as never before. The old lady recluse, who's probably never seen the light of day outside for years, is standing there, mouth open, staring-eyed, looking shrunken and untidy on the footpath. The new family at the corner is running in a graduated straggle round the corner, all eleven of them. As they vanish, the bloke next door and his wife with the new kid rush out. He's got the net and pole, and she has one arm full of kerosine tins and plastic bags, and one arm full of baby, and I swear it's not the former she's going to drop. I don't wait round looking anymore. Bugger the pole, I hive off through a short-cut down into Bright Street. And believe me, all ambulent Cobden seems to be there. I'm a heavy sleeper, late waker, and the street is now crowded with everyone before me, running, walking, staggering, hell for leather for the river.

Well, it's normally a ten-minute walk from my place to the bridge, but even with the crowd I make it in a three-minute run. After getting through the lame oldies and slow small fry, it's much easier of course. There was the risk of being skewered by poles, or having the breath thumped from one by a carelessly swung kero tin. Christchurch Friday-night-in-the-Square experience came to the fore here, though, and I'm in the van of the rush as we reach the river, that stretch just before the north end of the bridge.

Down the bank, trampling bush, slipping, kicking someone, grazing my hand on a tree I use to break my headlong eagerness a moment. All pulsing wild excitement to get a spot.

And stop aghast. Because, before God, the Grey is solid whitebait, bank to bank.

A fabulous mass of life, so thick in the river that water isn't seen. Just a seething froth of bait, frantic yet purposeful, a live river flowing in from the sea. And the hiss of disturbed water from their passing is louder than rain, louder than rapids, as spirited and loud as great falls.

I scoop, holding the rim of the net. It's FULL, absolutely chokka, and I drag it, elated, to the shore. The nylon is strained to its limits. Damn, nowhere to put the catch! But the bait, contrary to the normal lively whipping efforts to get out of the net and into the river, lie there like a sacrifice, and peacefully begin to die.

Strange. All my feverish desire to catch whitebait is gone. I lay the net with gentleness on the river-sand at my feet, and all along the bank, as the people come slithering excitedly down, and then stop, stunned, they are now doing the same. Over on the Greymouth side, the weird thing happens, as the crowds gather and swell and burst to the riverside. Horrified reverence for this impossible dream-run.

Except one man.

I don't know who he is, a thigh-booted dungareed individual, made distant and inhuman by his action. For he is swinging his net like an automaton, scooping the bait, flinging it silver and anywhere on to the shore. There is saliva hanging in a shining string from the corner of his mouth, and I am not so far away that I can't see the money-glaze on his eyes. It's inevitable, a feeling of disaster growing. Stop it you bastard, from voices in the crowd, leave them alone. But he continues shovelling up the unresisting harvest.

. . . an eddy in the river of bait, or an eddy of the crowd, pushing harder out? I don't know, but he is suddenly off his feet, falling with grotesque flailing slowness into the froth of eyes. The bait-river moves on, and how to swim when the water is gone, how to swim in a viscous moving jelly? His dark head is above the river once, shining all over the lucid bodies, mouth gaping open, nostrils flaring wide, but full of writhing fish. . . . If ever a man died in dream turned nightmare, that was him. And yet, not a movement or sound is heard from any of us. Just a shared feeling of wonderment, of rightness, and inevitability, as the whitebait we caught die on the shore. Things move to a conclusion.

And then there is an unforgettable sound, a vast wind of indrawn breath coming from the seaward end of the river. People astonished, bereft of all movement except the gasp of awe. Slowly it swells, welling along the banks of the river, both sides of the river, while we who have no knowledge, wait and there, mid-stream, lambent, borne on the living tide, the spirit of the waters, moving.

We disagreed how big today. Ten or maybe twelve feet of lighted perfection. Clear as the most clear water, except for the fine line of black speckling on his sides, and the slender dark-drawn rays of his four fins and tail . . . and the goldened brain in the top of his head . . . and the eyes, the great silver eyes, intensely circled black centres, burnished globes on the inward side of his head. They reflect neither intelligence nor love, nor malignity, but show forth pure being. Summation. A complete benign magnificence.

For as the multitude of whitebait had gathered to protect this one by sheer pacific numbers, so there was nothing to fear from him. Watch with calm incredulity as he passes.

King Bait.

And as much bait flowed behind in that protective solid wall, now unharried by fish or bird or man, as came to be preyed on before. I thought of the millions upon millions of ridiculous harmless little fish, who had been sacrificed to provide a safe passage for that majesty, and did not wonder much therefore at feeling echoes of their massed consuming joy.

There is nothing in the river, except the white slimefroth of their passing, and the water. And somebody says, loud in the quiet that follows after,

'Hell, I hope they make it to wherever that is going. I hope they get there.'

And somebody near me, voicing all the other thought of the people, 'God love us all, but are they ever coming back?'

I Say, Wait For Me

BARRY MITCALFE

I say, wait for me, he would call in that strange sort of English English we all somehow picked up when we went to college. He seemed slow on purpose, getting further and further behind, but it wasn't until the specialists, the X-rays, the many visits to the clinic that we found out why he was so awkward, crotchety and finicky. By then, it was almost too late. Almost but not quite. 'Sometimes it can take years, that is, if we can arrest it, but usually six to nine months, that's about all.' Surely the specialist didn't say that to me. It must be my father's voice. I remember many things from that time, clear pictures, slides of my mother and father kneeling and praying each side of silent and embarrassed Kevin, our minister saying that the Lord works in strange and mysterious ways, the lesson for to teach, humility is our lot. I remember Kevin, when we got home, playing war with me and our tin soldiers all over the hills and valleys his legs made in the bedclothes, and suddenly moving, swoosh, saying, that's the atom bomb, and I remember my mother standing behind. Just waiting and watching, or sitting in the easy chair on the verandah, sewing or reading or staring into space. She'd read a little, then would pause and an hour later you'd find her, still staring out, in a dream of her own.

I think she found it easier in the end, than any of us, to accept the will of the Lord God, the avenging Jehovah of my father's religion, because she had learnt submission, as a girl, as a woman; but not so with the rest of us.

His efforts to understand why the Lord should punish him put serious strains on my father's sanity, his fits of violent temper, his rages at things were one form of release. So was his passionate, firm and unforgiving insistence on church observance.

As one of the elders he had a duty, yes, but that did not mean that he should call on the Coulters each Monday to find why their Eileen hadn't attended church and then to insist on penances and a special service of intercession when what he had suspected proved true—that she was pregnant. He became a little mad about Sabbath observance too. He caught me sponging a stain on the heavy grey of my suit one Sunday morning, and there and then made me fall to my knees while he called on the Lord for guidance. Apparently the Lord guided him all right because I did not get the expected drubbing. He became sad, morose for days at a time, barely aware of our existence.

What hurt my father most, what gnawed at all of us, was that Kevin was such a terrific kid, I mean, too good to live, which is a horrible thing to say, but it did seem as if he were chosen of God, which didn't say much for God, so far as I was concerned. Kevin was a hell of a burden to me, I can tell you, because I'd been getting stuck into him one way and another, being a year older and feeling him always crowding hard on my heels. I was jealous of him, I guess, you know how it is, if you're older and stronger, it's as if you're put on earth as your brother's keeper, especially so when you know he hasn't got long to go.

I remember, one day he had taken all my *Popular Mechanics* and strewn them over the bed and the floor, sorting out the best way of making a motorised wheelchair so he could go anywhere round the house and garden. He'd drawn up a system of ramps and pulleys to get on and off the verandah, and he wanted to show it to me, but I'd had a lousy day at school. I'd been in trouble over some stupid little thing and when I came home and saw my carefully sorted magazines in such a mess I almost jumped on him, then, at the last moment remembered, the least movement was torture for him, so I burst out swearing instead. I hadn't known my mother was sitting there behind the door, but all she did was look terribly sad, and turn away from me when I said I was sorry. Later I heard Kevin arguing with her, saying, 'They're only words.' 'Only words—but you don't know what they mean!' 'They mean he was annoyed.' 'Oh, I suppose so,' she said reluctantly, but I noticed when I came in her face had lost that pinched, disgusted look, and she was able to smile when I said, 'Sorry I got mad, Kevin can have the P.M.s any time he likes.'

But that evening at tea, I had to sit and listen while my mother asked Divine Guidance for her son, so that he might follow the ways of righteousness which would bring him pure in heart and mind to your Cleansing Light, Oh Lord. Special for me. I just could not understand how my father and mother were still able to believe in such a God, a God who would let Kevin slowly die before their eyes. I was really curious about their belief. 'Is it the devil that's taking Kevin?' I asked my mother and she almost exploded. When my father heard what I'd said he was about to give me a walloping, then paused, asking 'Why did you say such a thing? You don't believe in the devil, do you?' 'If God is perfect, then surely the bad things must come from the devil,' I answered. My father stared at me in a puzzled, sort-of-surprised way. He really was a simpleton about some things. He forgot about the drubbing and I heard him saying to mum later, in tones of some wonder, 'James is developing into quite a religious thinker. Yes, quite a thinker.'

Little did they know how far beyond them I had gone in my thought—from believing in a devil that was more than holding his own in a war against God, to seeing both good and evil as man's work. Not many men—my father included—knew they had any real choice in the matter. It was man who made wars, murders, car accidents, hunger, pollution, all forms of unnecessary suffering. But Kevin, not Kevin, no, there was no answer to a thing like that. I was like my mother, too sad to think about it, but unlike her I did not, could not, accept it, not ever.

Strangely, the person who helped me most was Kevin. He would lie still, very still, in the mornings, on his bed in the verandah alcove. You wouldn't know he was awake until you saw his eyes, wide open and clear, clear as the sky in the window beyond his bed. He would spend hours just looking. I would sit and read, sometimes stopping to contemplate him, or to do as he was doing, sit staring into the sky's immensity.

'How many worlds are there?' he asked once. 'Worlds like ours?'

'Uncountable worlds,' I said.

He was quiet for a long time. I should have waited to hear his thoughts, but I rushed into the silence, trying to be the big brother. 'Every world is like a molecule, the biggest and the smallest things in nature are the same, they go round and round a nucleus.' My science wasn't the best for a fifth former, but at least it was my own.

'Perhaps the whole world has cancer.'

'What?'

'Cancer. Our world.'

'Oh? How do you make that out?'

'Men. We're a sort of cancer.'

'Who's been telling you that?'

'Nobody. Or rather Dr Abrahams. He told me about cancer cells not belonging. You know Jamie'—he always used that name for me—'man could be a sort of virus from out of space, like cancer, the spores just landed here, that's all.'

I was impressed by the idea, man *was* very recent on this earth and nobody really knew where or how he came, I mean, it could be true. I was a bit disconcerted to hear such ideas from my younger brother. 'Why do you say that?' I asked, non-committal.

'Well, man's different from everything else, I mean, he doesn't belong, he seems to change everything, I mean, look at New Zealand, look at what man's done in the short time he's been here.'

'What's he done?'

'Well, it was all bush and stuff before man came, strange animals, birds, plants. Now it's all dead wood and grass and cows and roads and things. Man comes—like a cancer.'

I didn't like him using that word. I was amazed at his courage, even more at his thought. He would lie there, not moving, but his mind would go racing far ahead of mine. I tried sometimes to put myself in his position, with only a short time to live, I didn't want to think about it. It would make me sick with guilt and relief that I was not him. I couldn't bear even to think of my own death away in some unknown time, but his so near, so precisely defined, how much more horrible.

I no longer looked for meaning in my parents' religion. My father was a lean, dark man, with black hair, a sallow complexion and glittering eyes. He was a lay preacher, very eloquent in a blood-and-thunder sort of style. I believe he would lie awake Saturday night composing his Sunday utterances or so my mother said, and it was true that sometimes we would wake and hear him pacing away the hours. He developed a prayer for Kevin, slowly perfecting it on several family occasions before his day as Lay Reader. 'Man that is born of woman has but a brief span on this earth,' he intoned, then gazed out under lowered brows to see how we were taking it. 'Our life is no more than the life of a flame on a candle, which devours until it is itself devoured. Therefore, oh Father, we ask that it burn clear and that it cast light, that all shall be brightened by its flame, that it consume not, nor itself be consumed in the everlasting fire to come. Oh Lord, heavenly Father, we ask it in your name. Amen.'

Brief but eloquent, my father, a convert to this particular brand of religion, where men and women sometimes spoke with tongues, where all human life was seen as the product of original sin and therefore tainted with the evil of its conception, lust and fleshly passion. This thought was a potent force in my formation, giving both a fear and a fascination about sex, a degree of self-mistrust that made my adolescence a peculiar form of purgatory. The sexual basis of my religion was stronger than the intellectual, I was taught that it was wrong simply to be me.

Yet I was lucky too, cleansed by an alien landscape that my father's overpowering sense of sin couldn't reach, down by the river where, in the old days, Kevin and the whole crowd of us would go on summer afternoons after school, diving into clear water and changing in the dark under the willows. It was there I'd had my first kiss, a fumbling affair with a black-haired girl called Katherine and it was there too, I think, Kevin fell for a girl called Ann-Marie, but of that I cannot be sure.

The very Sunday morning Kevin asked me to invite Ann-Marie and her brother, Richard—Kevin was too sick to go to church and I much to my secret relief, had to stay with him—my mother came home with Sister Bagnall who put on a special service at Kevin's bedside, with me, dad and two or three of mother's special friends. 'Suffer the little children to come unto me, in purity, in innocence, the children of the lamb shall rejoice before Thee,' on and on in that nasal, sing-song voice, which we called psalming. Oh, she was a great psalmer was Sister Bagnall; and then she called for the laying on of hands. 'Awful cold they were, too,' Kevin said afterwards, but all I could remember was the thin delicate skin stretched tight as parchment over his ribs and I couldn't laugh, even though Kevin had this physical self, like mine, and could laugh and shiver at a lot of silly old women playing their tricks, then ask me to bring the one girl, the girl he must have liked secretly without my knowing.

I knew he didn't care much for her brother, Richard, it was really Ann-Marie he wanted to see, but when they did come, after school on Tuesday, he spent most of the time talking to Richard and hardly even looked at Ann-Marie. She was a fourth former—I'd barely noticed her before, but she did have a nice look about her.

Kevin soon got tired and lay back, very pale. When mother

came and found him like that, she shooed us off. Ann-Marie and
Richard stopped to talk at the gate for a while. I'll never forget
coming back and finding Kevin haemorrhaging, all his pillow-
case and part of his sheet wet with bright, red blood.

Mother wouldn't let him go to hospital, she did the injections
and gave him the pills herself, but from then on he was rarely
awake, half-dozing, too weak to sit up. She would make him
drink soup through a straw and would bedpan him like a baby,
until she, too, had great, dark rings under her eyes—but not as
dark as his.

I think she never really believed in the same God after that,
how could she? 'Suffer the little children,' she said the morning
I found him staring out of sightless eyes at the bright, blue sky,
the sun rising on a day, a day like yesterday, but a day he
would never see. 'Suffer the little children,' it was said almost
as a reproach against a harsh and barren hillside of concrete
slabs and marble stones. Stony-eyed, she stood at the graveside.
Stony-eyed, beheld the empty world. But little by little she came
round, spent more and more time on church matters, served
on the Women's Guild, organised the Youth Drive, was the
mainstay of the meals-on-wheels and Forester Home for the
Aged, making peace with the Lord. And father, too, became
more devoted in his faith, his eyes would light with evangelical
zeal when he saw a backslider or soul to be won for the church.
He became one of the Friday night attractions at Pigeon Park,
the little strip of green between the Plaza and the Kings Theatre.
I used to slink past as if I'd never known him.

As for me, I broke away from home as soon as School C.
was over, driven into myself, knowing only the reality of those
thin ribs and our own impermanence, resolved therefore to live
more, if not better than before; like Mum and Dad, throwing
myself into life, Kevin's death a constant backdrop to our
every act.

Pigeons

HONE TUWHARE

When I came out of the pub, I had to stop and blink for a while before my eyes would come right. The road was drying out with steam rising and everything sparkled and shone. I decided to take a short-cut through the park and just then all the flowers in the garden began to perk up like they'd been waiting for somebody. Anybody. But I walked past them and between the flower-beds like I was a captured General, not looking, and with my mind somewhere else. I had sold only three copies of the paper.

Pigeons were walking tight circles around the old man sitting on the park seat, like they were crafty sheep-dogs circling one way, and then the other.

'Gidday,' I said, flourishing my bundle of Communist papers. 'Would you like to know who is behind COMALCO, eh?'

The old man lifted a vague but cautionary hand without looking at me.

'Don't make any sharp movements,' he said, watching the pigeons. 'I think they're getting leaner every year. . . .'

'Yeah well,' I said, making talk. 'Maybe there's fewer of you fellahs around to feed them, eh?'

'Nah: that's not it,' he said, looking at me briefly.

Carefully, I placed a folded copy of the paper down by his side.

'I remember the Depression,' he said, looking sideways at the paper but not touching it.

'I been through the big War too,' he said. 'I reckon I knocked off a couple of Nazis. . . . But you know, it hasn't made much difference, all that.'

Hell, I thought, he'll be giving me his life history next. I'd better move on to the next pub.

When a kid on a crazy bicycle shot in among them, the pigeons rose easily up in the air in a great swirl of feathers ready to bomb indiscriminately. But instead they hovered and wheeled down invisible motor-ways, clover-leaved, like they were the original architects with the runway right there at the old man's feet. And all of a sudden I got very generous. Reaching into my rucksack, I began to break up a wedge of chocolate biscuits chucking some of the broken bits at the pigeons.

'You didn't have to do that,' said the old man. 'You are spoiling them. . . .'

'Oh well,' I said, kind of helpless. 'Here, you feed them.' And dropping the biscuits on the seat, I began to edge away.

'How much does the red rag cost these days?' he asked.

'Eight cents.'

'Too much,' he said. 'Here's five.'

I took the money.

When I reached the other side of the park, I looked back. The old man looked as if he was reading chocolate biscuits and munching the paper. The pigeons had moved in close and were pecking new lace-holes in his scrubbed shoes.

Making Father Pay

FRANK SARGESON

Strangers were sometimes in doubt which was the father and which the son. A slight figure cut off short, with snowy hair that went well with smooth red-apple cheeks, father would never see ninety again. He was Old Charlie. Twenty years behind him (and for that reason Young Charlie), his son was an astonishing copy, except that a mild look of worry replaced the repose of the older man's features. Or was it that *his* apples were wrinkled as though gathered from the grass instead of picked fresh from the tree.

Once upon a time there had been the old lady to keep an eye on the pair of them. But years ago she had as you might say left her son to carry the baby—and because of father's eccentric behaviour the expression is apt. Long retired from a business partnership, he was said to be very well-off, although in these long latter years there was nobody to say he had ever been seen to spend money—but that is to say apart from the single exception of a bout of paint-buying. The intention had been that Young Charlie, who in his day had been a painter and paperhanger, would do the house up. Nothing had ever come of it, but the paint remained stacked in many out of the way corners: and in any case all was forgotten when the old man became devoted to fishing.

It is, however, doubtful whether that last word is the right one—for despite his daily angling, this fisherman was never deterred by the absolute lack of any trace of stream lake pond or sea within at least half a mile from where he sat with rod line float and baited hook. Seated on his little wooden stool he fished the little front lawn. And since the suburb was seaside, and as such inhabited by a great variety of amateur fishermen, there were many citizens to stop and look in at the gateway through the thick high wall of hedge: there would be waggish comment besides good advice about how to catch the fish that appeared to be fished for. It was generally believed to be piper the old man must be after, the more especially as there was no mistaking the gentles he from time to time baited his hook with: wriggling and writhing, they made the oatmeal in the jam jar at his feet look very much alive.

It is not my purpose to suggest any rational explanation for the old man's eccentric behaviour: sufficient to say that besides appearing to spend his daylight hours in a most satisfying occupation, he enjoyed good health and ate and slept well: also he seemed never to hear the advice, the funny comments and questions so very often directed towards him from over the front gate.

But what began eventually to happen in the mind of his son is perhaps another matter.

For a good part of each day Young Charlie would sit on the verandah. Clearly he was keeping an eye on the old man, but it might also have been noted that the paperbacks he read would often concern themselves with the question of somebody's mysterious disappearance. And a sharp observer might have noticed it was the same thing with a good many newspaper items (and indeed, not so long after the events of my story there were those who remembered a tavern-occasion when the whereabouts of a certain Mr Tufnell-Turner were discussed: he was the missing inhabitant of a topcrust suburb, a very helpless, very aged man who had quite unaccountably disappeared: and when it was Young Charlie's turn to say what he thought about the mystery he hadn't hesitated: 'It's easy, his old lady ate him.' But this macabre solution was too much: exclamations were followed by uneasy laughter, and then silence).

Also, there was afterwards almost nobody to dispute that about this time Young Charlie's look of worry seemed to be mysteriously erased from his features. It was as though he must have found a new interest in life—and yet, quite surprising when he continued to complain to neighbours and tavern-cronies about the burden his aged parent could be. But there was sympathy. It was remembered that in the old man's much younger days, long before the era of over-population, he had owned a large empty block of land in what was now a busy crowded suburb: yet always it had been said his hand was tight upon the purse-strings: it was believed he had been reluctant to lend a hand to his bachelor son in the difficult times of that long-ago Slump when house-painting jobs were simply not to be had. And to descend to petty matters—it was no secret to near neighbours that harsh words were sometimes heard upon the subject of gentles: there had always to be a good-sized lump of rotten meat strung up in the lemon tree just outside the kitchen door—to be flyblown, and so ensure a good supply of gentles for regular transfer to the fattening oatmeal of the jam jar. There were times when the voice of Young Charlie could be heard several doors away: his curses were for smells flies maggots and old men.

But as a topic of conversation, what was soon to become even more interesting than the effacement of Young Charlie's look of worry, was father's own sudden transfigured appearance. Nothing could be done about snow on his head, or cheeks like red apples, nor was anything called for (it would be to interfere with perfection), but the clothing he had worn on and on since the time of the old lady had become more and more a shabby disgrace. Sudden transformation was at first almost not to be believed; and since the old man never left the property, clearly all had been up to Young Charlie. Overnight father had ceased to be a drab old man—had become instead a most enchanting garden gnome: animated however, and the fishing instead of being absurd was now absolutely right. And so were the colours. Nobody had supposed that Young Charlie could prove himself so signally yet secretly gifted with such splendid imagination. Red woollen cap with gold tassel, green pullover, dark-blue corduroy trousers which tucked into multi-coloured shining boots—the figure was one which might be fancifully thought to belong among the magic signs of the zodiac. And from the comments of appreciating citizens who looked in over the gate, you could readily infer there would be no disagreement.

But in the event there appeared to be no doubt it had been no part of Young Charlie's serious intentions to put his father on public view all dressed in his finery—not as a free show, and not just yet anyway. It had not, as it were, been opening day, and the preview was quickly put an end to.

Nor was it until some months had elapsed (and the front gateway was so effectively boarded up nobody could look in any more), that Young Charlie had completed his preparatory labours: and because of the great thick dividing hedges neighbours had not been able to see in either, nor for the most part had there been anything unusual to hear—and indeed, it had seemed that even harsh words about smells or whatever had for the time being ceased. But for all that there had been a fine and beautiful morning when a great lorry, with a huge slowly revolving bowl of certified concrete mixture, had pulled up outside the back gate. It had afterwards gingerly backed on to the property: and before departing had also delivered a labour-saving machine for spraying liquid cement on appropriate surfaces.

But all was surmise until the day when two passing fishermen were astonished to see that a bell had been fixed to the boarded-up front gateway, with a notice attached which said, PLEASE RING TO SEE GARDEN ORNAMENT. ENTRANCE PRICE 5C.

Young Charlie answered the bell, and afterwards the two citizens agreed the charge was not excessive. Old Charlie was not of course on view, but the fishing gnome was magnificent, a work of art if ever there was one. Young Charlie's drinking friends had all many times been told about the paint stored in the house for so many years—and what marvellous use had now been made of it! There it all was, red cap and gold tassel, red cheeks, green torso, and the trunk lower down a dark-blue . . . all solid shining fresh, yes, fresh as paint! And of course fishing! And what was so very marvellous, the final triumph so to speak, all (as every good work of art always should be) that little bit extra to life-size.

Who can doubt that someday the cops will catch up on the culprit?—and I have myself seen one of them rest his elbow on the top of the red cap while he inquires from Young Charlie when he expects his father to return from a protracted visit to a brother in Australia. But who can know exactly all that he had to put up with in the lifetime of the old man?—who of course had to go sometime anyhow. Sometimes I imagine a moment before the cement covered his eyes—a sudden look in them which said, 'Thank you, son—thank you for conferring upon me this Immortality.'

Meantime lots of people, visitors, tourists and the rest, find it worthwhile to pay the five cents.

Rural Delivery

JOY COWLEY

The boy lay across the back seat of the station wagon, counting the bends in the road by the pressure on his feet or the top of his head. He was wearing felt slippers over woollen socks but his head was bare, hot and slightly aching, and when his father made a fast left turn the weight on his skull made white lights in front of his eyes.

His eyes hurt more than his head or throat in spite of the dullness of the day. If he stared at the window too long the lines of rain scratched him through the glass and he had to pull the blanket over his face to find darkness.

He had felt like this yesterday at school but it had seemed worse then with the noise of the classroom, questions pecking at him from every direction, and finally the crying with eyes and nose running down his arm and on to the desk.

Today he had his father's handkerchief.

Lying flat against the pillow he was unable to see his father in the driver's seat, but the stops were frequent, sometimes less than a minute apart, and each time his father got out there was some joke about ducks or mud, or a story about the farmer whose name appeared on the mailbox. For a moment his father's face would be large above him, laughing and spilling drops of rain, then the door would slam and he'd be pressed back in the seat with the sound of water rushing under the tyres.

Bread, newspapers, green canvas bags of mail, even through his cold they reached him, not as separate odours but one which was as warm and personal as the smell inside his schoolbag.

'Dad?' He had been forbidden to sit up. He put his hands behind his head and raised it until he could see the yellow hood of his father's parka. 'Hey Dad?'

'What?'

'You know at school that Jason Morris, he said I was a liar. He said nobody's been on every road in New Zealand. Like I was just skiting.' He swallowed to wet his throat. 'I told him he was dumb. I said it was even the little roads not on the maps and the ones that only went halfway to places. That's right, isn't it Dad? You went on every single one?'

'You bet your sweet life I did.' His father slapped both hands on top of the steering wheel and straightened his arms, pushing back against the seat. 'The whole lot, Chief. Every road in the country right down to Stewart Island where they all wear grass skirts and hardly know what a car looks like. That kid in school, you tell him to stick a pin in the map—anywhere, you tell him—and I'll show him my own personal tread marks.'

'And not just trucks, eh Dad? Big artics and petrol tankers and ready-mix concrete—'

'Every one of them Chief. I've carried anything and everything on just about any set of wheels you'd care to name. Including people, of course, and that I reckon's the hardest by a long chalk, a bus-load of people. Oh, it'd all be fine enough if you had that little green man driving alongside you, but if he wasn't there, then that was it, Chief, that was when you wished you had a crate of steers or a load of old potatoes. I tell you I'd rather drive a petrol tanker through a forest fire than be stranded with a busful of human souls. Specially tourists. Don't talk to me about tourist coaches. I've seen them all and there were things happened that'd make me sob again in the telling. Saints alive! Now look what we've done!'

He braked so suddenly that the boy hurt his elbow against the door handle. The engine whined in reverse and the tail of the station wagon slewed towards a white mail-box. There were black letters on it but it was a long name and the boy's eyes got sore before he could work it out.

'That was close,' said his father. 'You wouldn't get a meaner old devil than this one. If I forgot his bread and paper, you know what he'd do, don't you? Set his bull on me. And heaven preserve us, you've never seen horns the likes of that before. Great brute of a thing. It'd rip this buggy open like a can of spaghetti in two seconds flat.'

'You're kidding,' said the boy. He pulled the blanket up round his chin, partly because of the draught from the open door, and sat up. In front of him there was a driveway with a house set far back in a clump of trees. On either side the paddocks were flat and full of sheep which nibbled grass as though they didn't know it was raining. Only a few near the road bothered to lift their heads and stare.

The boy's father opened the mail-box, threw in a loaf and a newspaper, closed it again, all with a quick crackle of yellow sleeve.

Rain was pencilled over everything. The driveway was flooded, a hump of clay and grass between two lines of brown water. Along the hump several geese waddled towards the house.

The boy turned his head. A blackbird landed on the post near his window, flicked its tail, flew away again. There was no sign of the bull. He yawned and lay back, his head fitted into the dent on his pillow, and counted the sweeps of the windscreen wipers. He was good at counting. He could count better than anyone else in his class.

Eighty-seven, eighty-eight—he raised his head again. 'You wait. I'm going to tell that Jason Morris it's him that's the liar.'

'Who?' said his father.

'Jason Morris. That kid at school—you know.'

'Oh, him.' His father nodded slowly. 'I know how you feel, Chief. Believe me, I know. But a liar's an awful bad thing to call a man. If I were you I'd just rest content with the knowing of it. Like what your mother used to say. When people talk bad about others, she said, it wasn't others they was judging but themselves. I'd go along with that, Chief. I'd reckon it wasn't too far out.'

The boy stared at the window and counted until the light made him blink. 'I told the kids at school my mother was dead.'

His father's head turned. 'Why in God's name?'

'Dunno.'

'Ah—come on now. You'd have to remember why you said a thing like that.'

'I don't know. I just did. I just said it.'

'David, there has to be a reason. People don't go around saying their mothers are dead when they're not. That's terrible. I mean, supposing she were to hear about it. How do you think she'd feel? Her own son talking her down into the grave like that—'

'She won't. You said she went back to Ireland.'

'There's ways people have of finding out even if they're on the other side of the earth. You shouldn't have said it. I've told you before, time and time again, there's things you won't understand until you're well growed up—'

The boy wished he'd kept quiet. He hadn't realised his father would make such a fuss, nor did he know why he'd told his classmates she was dead. There had been no good reason— except that it was easy to say.

His father stopped talking about it at the next mail-box and after that started making jokes again. He began his whistling too, not ordinary tunes but bird calls, warbles, high-pitched trills, his cheeks going in and out like the throat of a thrush. The boy sat up within range of the rear vision mirror and when he knew he'd been seen, he edged forward and put his arms across the top of his father's seat. As they braked at the entrance of another driveway, he asked if he could come through to the front.

'You're not supposed to be sitting up at all,' said his father. 'Lie down.'

'Oh Dad!'

'Go on now, lie right down like I said. You know what'll happen? You'll have a dreadful seizure and your face'll get hotter than hell, so hot your brain'll melt like a little icecream and run out your nose.'

'It won't!'

'Won't it just? I wouldn't be too smart if I were you. See now, you're getting redder all the time.' He put out his hand and rested his palm on the boy's forehead. 'You feeling all right?'

'I'm okay,' said the boy.

'Hungry?'

He shook his head.

'How about thirsty?'

The boy nodded.

'I'll get you a drink. That lunch stop I mentioned, it's only a few miles away. Six more deliveries, then I'll get you anything you fancy—orange, milk, lemonade, you only have to say.'

The boy put his hand in his dressing gown pocket. 'I brought my own money.'

'Money?' His father laughed. 'Saints alive, there's no shop out here. Did you think I meant a shop? There's not as much as a service station in these parts. No, this is just a place where I have my lunch now and then.' As he started to drive again, he said, 'You'll get on well with her. She's a good sort.'

'Who?' said the boy.

'The lady who gives us lunch, of course. She's got a lot of dogs down there. You'll hear them yapping their heads off before we're anyway stopped—big ones, little ones, some of the funniest breeds you ever set eyes on.'

The boy lay back on the pillow. 'Do you go there lots?'

'No. Once or twice. It's too bad you've got the snuffles or you could be having a good look round the kennels. There's one dog with so much hair on it, you don't know which end is which, and that's a fact.'

'Tell me about the buses,' said the boy.

'Which ones?'

'You know. About tourists and things that happen.'

'Oh that,' said his father. 'You mean when the little green man deserts you in the middle of the night on the Lewis Pass with your power steering gone and six foot of snow and 38 Japanese who don't have a word of the Queen's English amongst them? Is that what you mean?'

'Yes, yes.' He propped himself up on one elbow. 'Tell me about that.'

'Well—it's an awful long story, Chief, a good eight-miler, I'd say. And the telling of it would be terrible thirsty work. We'll keep it for the road home.'

'Tell me a little story.'

'Not on an empty stomach.'

'Please? Dad?'

'After lunch.'

The boy lay down and turned his face to the back seat. His stomach itched. He kicked the blanket away but was still too hot. And when he scratched his stomach, it hurt.

'She's a nice lady,' said his father. 'You tell her what you want—a lemonade, coke, chocolate milk—and she'll get it for you. You'll like her.'

The boy said nothing. He reached for the blanket, pulled it over his head and lay still, pretending to sleep.

Perhaps he did doze a minute or two, for the woman's voice came on him suddenly, surprising him out of someplace hot and distant. They were no longer moving. The engine had stopped and so had the drumming of rain. There was only her voice coming in from outside, touching him until he was listening.

'He should be in bed,' she was saying. 'On a day like this? Oh Joe, you must be out of your mind.'

'I couldn't leave him on his own. The lady who looks after

him Saturday mornings, she's working, you see. I didn't have any choice.'

The boy kept his eyes closed as his father drew the blanket back from his face.

'He's very flushed.' The woman's voice was closer.

'He's got a real snorter, but I wrapped him up warm enough. He'll come to no harm.'

'He's too warm. Have you taken his temperature? Joe, he's burning up. It's more than a cold. Look—how long's he had that redness behind the ears?'

'First I've noticed. Looks like a bit of a rash.'

'Measles,' she said.

'You reckon?' His father was pulling at the blanket again. 'Come on Chief, wake up. There's a lad, roll over and let's have a good look at you.'

The boy groaned and fluttered his eyelids.

'I say it's German measles,' said the woman.

'David?' said his father.

'What?' The boy decided to wake up. His father was kneeling on the front seat and leaning over him. He looked different, his hair combed, the grey jersey instead of the yellow parka, and he was talking a different way—as though he had borrowed someone else's voice and was being very careful with it. The woman watched through the half open window. Her hair was done in pigtails but she was old, about thirty, and she wore a shirt with cowboys and lassos on it.

It wasn't raining.

'David, this is Mrs Turner, the lady I was telling you about.'

'You poor kid,' she said. 'That's what it is. You've got measles.'

'Mrs Turner's getting you that drink. And what about a bite to eat now? A sandwich?'

The boy shook his head.

'He won't want to eat,' said the woman. 'Plenty of liquids, that's what he needs. Diluted orange juice with glucose.' She looked at the boy. 'Do you want ice in it, David?'

He nodded.

The boy's father was opening the back door. 'Now don't try to walk or anything funny, Chief. That's what dads are for. Roll yourself tight in the rug—'

'You can't bring him inside,' said the woman.

The boy's father looked at her.

'It's German measles, Joe. I've never had German measles. I'm sorry, he can't come into the house.'

'It's not the flaming smallpox!' his father said in his own voice.

'Nearly as bad,' she said.

'But you're not—you know.'

'What's that got to do with it?' She turned to the boy. 'You understand, David, what you've got is very catching. I mean very, very catching. You feel bad enough, but when adults get it, it's a whole lot more serious. Much worse. David, I'm going to get some orange drink for you. And your father's sandwiches. And I'm bringing them out here to the car. Then I think your father should take you straight home.'

The boy's father scratched the back of his neck and looked as though he was going to laugh. 'Now wait a minute. Look, we haven't got ourselves any problem. I'll bring his drink out and then we'll have lunch inside, the two of us.'

'Leave David out here on his own?'

'We'll not exactly be deserting him. Will we, Chief? I mean, we'll be sitting in the kitchen not ten yards away.'

'You can't,' she said. 'You can't leave him.'

'He stayed outside the Post Office while I sorted the mail this morning,' he said.

'Joe, it's not right,' she said and she turned away.

'What can possibly happen—'

'I'm sorry,' she said.

The boy's father stood at the rear of the wagon staring after her, while the boy counted her footsteps. As she moved beyond his window he stopped counting to ask, 'Can I sit up now?'

'I suppose so,' said his father.

They had parked close to a large house. On either side were white painted walls and, in front, a carport containing a blue Volkswagon and a mud spattered motor bike. The woman was walking through the side of the carport to a brown door.

For the first time the boy became aware of the barking of dogs. There must have been dozens of them and yet they were so far away they sounded like a chorus of insects. 'Where are the kennels?' he asked.

His father didn't answer. He was staring at the house and softly tapping his fingers on the roof of the station wagon, his eyes half-shut as though he were dreaming.

'I can hear the dogs,' said the boy.

His father stopped tapping and smiled at him. He came inside and sat on the edge of the seat, one leg still out the door.

'Feeling better already, aren't you?'

The boy smiled back.

'I told you she was a nice lady.'

The boy nodded. He put his hand inside his dressing gown and scratched his stomach.

'Now look, Chief, you and me—we both know that fair's fair. You wouldn't want me missing out on a decent lunch just because you're sick. And you heard what she said. I did my best but she doesn't want you in there while you got the measles. That's fair too. But I don't have the measles, do I now?'

The boy shook his head.

'And I know *you* won't object if I have a decent lunch sitting at a table.'

He shook his head again. 'I don't mind.'

'It's her,' his father said. 'You know how women are about these things. They make an awful fuss at times. I think you'll have to tell her when she comes out. Will you, Chief? Just say you're quite all right and you want to go to sleep. You need the rest. Tell her it's not easy sleeping on these bumpy roads. Can you remember that?'

The boy nodded.

'For your old Dad?'

'Yes,' said the boy.

His father ruffled his hair. 'I'll see what's keeping her,' he said.

The boy watched as he marched across the yard towards the door at the end of the carport, wide steps, hands in pockets, whistling. He went into the house without knocking, closed the door behind him.

No sound came from the house but beyond it, almost at the edge of listening, the barking and yelping of dogs never stopped for an instant.

The boy watched the brown door, counting to make it open. At one-hundred-and-seventy-one they both came out together, his father carrying at tray, laughing a lot, talking in that voice, and she a bit behind him with her head down.

His father came up to the wagon and beckoned the boy to look. 'What did I tell you?' he laughed, showing a white cloth, a paper napkin, a glass and a plastic jug full of juice with pips at the bottom and ice cubes on the top.

The woman walked to the other side of them but didn't come too close. She stooped to window level. 'Yes, I think you are a bit better. Less like a boiled beet. Perhaps it was the blanket round your face. Is your throat dry? Poor kid, I'll bet you've got a raging thirst.'

She was right. He drank two glasses of the juice straight off, gulping and gasping, scarcely tasting it. His father poured a third and said, 'Does that make a difference?'

He took the glass and fished out a pip, then he sipped with his face down over the rim.

'How do you feel now?'

He didn't answer.

'Good, eh? I'll bet that's the sweetest drink you've ever tasted. You know how many oranges got squeezed to make that lot?'

Without a word the boy handed back the still full glass. He glanced at the woman. She wasn't looking at him but at his father, shaking her head and rounding her mouth to the shape of no.

'He's fine, he just told me. Didn't you, Chief?'

The boy was silent.

'He said all he wanted was a bit of a snooze. Right, David? Isn't that what you told me?'

'Joe, stop bullying the boy!'

'I'm not bullying him, for heaven's sake. Hey! Cat got your tongue? Tell her. Tell her what you told me. What was it you said about wanting to go back to sleep?'

The boy didn't look at his father. He started to cough and the tears came, prickling at first, then a real flow as the coughing hurt his throat. He put his arms across his stomach and rocked back and forth. 'I want to go home.'

For a moment no one said anything; then his father put the glass back on the tray and handed it to the woman. She took the tray at arm's length and said, 'Just the jug. Joe, you take the glass.'

'Oh bloody hell!' said his father. He reached across the tray and tipped the orange juice out on the ground, then he brought his arm back and threw the glass right over the carport roof.

The boy didn't hear it land.

The woman tidied the things on the tray as though the glass had never been there, while the boy's father got into the car and started the engine.

'Joe, you'll let me know, won't you?' called the woman.

'Don't worry,' he shouted back. 'I'll let you know all right.'

She stood in front of the carport and watched as they reversed down the drive. The boy thought he might wave, and would have if his father had, but instead he held on to the back of the front seat with both hands.

At the end of the drive his father turned the wheels in a spray of muddy water, then took off so fast that the boy was pushed down on to the back seat. He lay where he had fallen for a while, then he got up on one elbow and said, 'I felt sick.'

'Sure,' said his father.

'I felt as sick as anything.' He moistened his lips. 'You know what? I got spots all over my stomach.'

His father didn't comment.

The boy sat up and undid his dressing gown, then his pyjama jacket. He pulled up his vest and touched the red lumps on his skin. He had them everywhere, millions of them all over his body. He fastened his buttons again. 'Dad?'

A grunt came from the front seat.

'What about that time in the bus?'

'What about it?' said his father.

'You were going to tell me.'

There was a pause. 'I've forgotten.'

'No you haven't. About the little green man and the time you got stuck in the snow.'

'What little green man?' His father's voice was angry. 'There's no such thing as a little green man. That's a load of old rubbish!'

The boy leaned sideways to look at his father's face in the rear vision mirror. He watched it for a while, then he lay down on the seat with his pillow and blanket, and counted. After a few miles he went to sleep.

An Inquiry into the Construction and Classification of the New Zealand Short Story

A. K. GRANT

The short story and the poem are the two forms in which New Zealand writers have achieved the greatest distinction. What is not generally appreciated is that, while on the one hand only a rare spirit can write a good poem, on the other hand almost any literate person can write a good New Zealand short story. The reason for this is that there is a finite number of types of New Zealand short story. Their skeletons have been assembled by pioneers and all the modern writer has to do is flesh them out. In support of my thesis I shall list below a number of basic, irreducible types of New Zealand short story, accompanied by suggestions as to the development of the possibilities with which each is pregnant.

(1) *The sensitive Maori kid who doesn't quite know what is going on short story . . .*

Such short stories, as their categorisation suggests, commonly involve a Maori boy of about ten years of age, around whom things happen which he grasps but dimly. They frequently begin as follows:

Watene sat on the wooden steps of the back door. He could smell the odour of the kumara scones his mother was baking in the kitchen. Outside, his father was tinkering with the engine of the 1937 Ford V8 which his father called The Old Sow. Watene laughed, thinking of his father calling the Old

Sow the Old Sow. The sun warmed his limbs. Watene felt good.

Following the opening passages of this type of story, an Event occurs. The Event is followed in due course by its acceptance by the child protagonist, even though he doesn't understand it properly. Alternatively the c.p. accepts and throws his arms around an adult who precipitated or was involved in the event. The whole story should be redolent of the odour of Polynesian sanctity and should condemn by implication the lapsed, unspontaneous nature of the Pakeha, unable to respond to simple events in a simple way.

(2) *The Ordinary Kiwi working bloke short story . . .*

A lot of these were written during the thirties and forties. They are narrated in the first person by an Ordinary Kiwi working bloke who explains why one of his workmates drives him up the wall and tells us what he does about it. One should leap straight into the mise-en-scène when writing such a story:

I knew there was going to be trouble as soon as Fred, our foreman, brought Mortimer over. Mortimer looked a real nong. 'This here is Mortimer,' said Fred. 'He's a pongo, but he can't help it.' He walked away, rolling a smoke between his left ear and the side of his head without using his hands. None of us could work out how he did it. 'Grab hold of that bloody grubber,' I said. 'What's a grubber?' asked Mortimer, like a nong. 'Oh dear, oh bloody dear,' I said to myself.

This type of story can develop in two ways: (a) Mortimer proves not to be such a nong after all and is eventually, though grudgingly, accepted by the narrator; (b) he really does prove to be trouble and something bad happens—a fight, a work accident—as a consequence of which the gang breaks up and the narrator slopes off back to the big smoke. In order to give the story an historical perspective the incident should occur during the Depression but its narration should be taking place ten or twenty years later. This allows the narrator to append a coda along the following lines:

One afternoon in Queen Street I bumped into Shorty, who had been in the gang with us. I took him to the Prince of Wales, bought him a few pony beers, and we yarned about old times. 'What ever happened to Mortimer?' I asked him. 'Haven't you heard?' said Shorty, incredulous. 'Morty's just landed a $5 million contract selling wood chips to the

Japanese.' I didn't say anything. I simply moved on to the top shelf.

(3) *Then if you think you're depressed already just wait till you read this but it may help me to make some sense of my breakdown short story . . .*

This type of short story is directly related to the confessional poetry of Robert Lowell, Anne Sexton and Sylvia Plath. The creative impetus behind it more commonly finds its expression in the form of a novel rather than a short story. However short stories of this type do appear. I shall not give an example of one because I am feeling quite cheerful, a frail mood and one easily dispelled by contemplation of the type of short story I am refusing to contemplate.

(4) *The loveable housewife and mother coping with adolescent kids in the suburbs short story . . .*

This is much the most meritorious type of New Zealand short story because unlike all the others it does not preserve itself in the aspic of its own solemnity. It was developed almost single-handed by Marie Bullock and begins as follows:

I wandered into the front room. George, my eldest, was lying on the sofa eating a Vegemite sandwich with one hand and plucking at the strings of his guitar with the other. 'Have you done your chemistry homework?' I asked. 'No,' said George. 'Chemistry's stupid.' What could I say? I agreed with him. 'Well go and tidy up your bedroom,' I riposted feebly. 'Don't need to,' said George smugly. 'I've given Donny ten cents to do it.' 'Donny!' I cried. 'But he's only three!' 'So what?' said George. 'He still knows what ten cents is worth.'

(5) *The zonked out of one's skull in Ponsonby short story . . .*

The zonked out of one's skull in Ponsonby short story was developed in the sixties and production models appear in our literary magazines to this very day. In such short stories the writer attempts to combine the described sexual and hallucinogenic experience without making sense of either and using words rather than language, for example:

. . . cast off cried the red admiral I put my hands under her buttocks while the heliotrope wall flowed into the Propontis push she cried but I floated bobbing against the stars bobbing prodding oh god oh god yes her heels fused with my calves and we soared into a mauve Van Allen belt while she came out of the unknown I could keep this kind of stuff up forever but you will have taken my point by now . . .

(6) *The sub-Katherine Mansfield 'At the Bay' short story* . . .
The first rays of the sun slid over the peak of Mt Winterslow and stabbed downward to a dew-drop trembling on the tip of a toitoi plume. A faint breeze stirred the top branches of the tall beech tree on the edge of the school playground. Fantails flicked about the branches looking for all the world as though they were attached to the trunk by invisible strands of elastic. An opalescent mist rose—oh so uncertainly!—from the long grass beside the shingle road. The dust of the road had been dampened by the dew and smelled of dew-dampened dust. In the paddock next to the school two horses cropped the wet grass with a sound like pinking shears cutting through velvet.

In a corner of the playground stood a square white tent. The flaps on one side had been folded right back. In front of the tent two wooden trestles supported a large flat board. For now the tent was empty, but soon it would be full of teachers noting results and parents inquiring about placings.

It was the day of the school sports.

The above list is not, of course, exhaustive. There are at least four other basic types of short story which I have not listed because I write such stories myself. None have so far been accepted for publication. I am aware of the reason for this. All that stands between my short stories and the acknowledgment of a major new talent is the lack of a suitable non-de-plume. A. K. Grant carries no aura or penumbra with it. O. E. Middleton suggests intelligence, Maurice Shadbolt combines the Gallic artiness of Maurice with the no-nonsense Anglo-Saxon sound of Shadbolt, Frank Sargeson is suitably demotic, Katherine Mansfield is the sort of name you would expect a sensitive upper middle-class spirit to have. A. K. Grant—there's just nothing there. I think I might try Peregrine Ruapehu de Vere Stacpoole Whineray.